NOT SORRY

ELLA MILES

1

SEAN

I DON'T KNOW what the hell I'm doing here. I promised I would never come back to Chicago. It's too damn cold here. Still, I find myself stepping off a plane at O'Hare International Airport in Chicago. Why?

Because I'm an idiot.

And, when Jamie Parks calls me, saying she needs help, I come running. I would do anything for that girl, and she knows it, including marrying her, if she would only say yes. But I know that's not in the cards for us. It's been over a year since the last time I saw her. I'm just hoping she'll let me take her on a date after I help her save her real estate company.

I wheel my carry-on bag through the airport and out to Arrivals where Jamie said she would pick me up, but I don't see Jamie waiting for me anywhere. I sigh. Jamie always used to run late.

I pull my phone out of my pocket and get started on answering emails and returning daily phone calls to check in with my company. I pace back and forth as I talk, trying to stay warm, which is impossible due to the snow and cold wind that are whipping around the side of the airport and hitting me straight in the face over and over again.

Fuck this.

I head back into the airport to wait for Jamie. I text her that I'm just inside Arrivals and then continue doing work until she gets here.

I hang up on my latest call and glance at the time. She's over forty minutes late. This is getting ridiculous. I should have just taken a cab to her office.

The doors slide open, letting in another burst of cold air that I'm getting more than annoyed with, but there isn't anywhere else for me to wait. I glance at the woman standing in the doorway, hoping it's Jamie, but I immediately realize that it isn't.

Still, I continue to stare at the woman in the doorway, transfixed with how much of a giant mess she is. She's wearing dark snow boots that look white from the snow that is covering them. Her legs are shivering because, for some crazy reason, she decided not to wear pants or tights or those yoga pant things women usually wear. And she is wearing the smallest yet puffiest pink coat I've ever seen. In her hand, she is carrying a cup of coffee from what I assume is a local coffee shop because I don't recognize the brand on the side of the cup.

She nervously glances around the room and then smiles when she sees me. She walks over to me, and I think she is going to ask for directions or how an airport works because she looks completely out of place here. Hopefully, she is traveling someplace warm, which would explain her bare legs. I will admit, those legs do look hot—long and lean, just like I like. I guess it would be a waste of good legs if she covered them.

"Are you Sean?" the woman asks.

My eyes widen a bit in shock, partially from the fact that she knows my name and partially when I see that she is wearing makeup on only about half of her face. I laugh a little at the sight. I can't help it. But then the door opens, and another breeze of cold air pushes through us. Her long, frizzy dark hair blows in her face, and my nose breathes in her sweet smell. *Apples and cherries maybe?*

This woman is clearly having an off day. I hope it's an off day because I can't imagine anyone going through life every day like this. But, underneath all of the mess, something has me intrigued.

"Yes, although no one calls me that."

"Oh, I'm sorry. Jamie didn't tell me that you went by a nickname."

I shake my head, chuckling a little bit. "I don't go by a nickname."

"Oh." She frowns, unsure of what I mean.

"I go by Mr. Burrows."

She bites her lip. "I'm sorry, Mr. Burrows. I'm just so happy I found you. You have no idea about the morning I've had."

I snicker as I look her up and down and cock my head to one side. "I have a pretty good idea."

She blushes. "Anyway, I'm Olive. I'll be driving you to the Parks Real Estate office."

I frown. Jamie couldn't even bother to come pick me up.

"It's so nice to meet you, Mr. Burrows," Olive says as she leans forward.

I have no idea what she is doing. I assume she has to tell me something privately, so I lean forward a little, too, and the next thing I know, her lips graze my cheek before brushing against my lips.

I smile when her soft lips touch mine. I assume she is passing along a greeting from Jamie, and her lips are very nice. I will never turn down a kiss.

But, the next moment, I feel hot coffee all over my body, and

I look up to see a blushing Olive with a cup of coffee in her hand that I'm sure is empty now.

"Oh my God. I'm so, so sorry. I didn't mean to spill coffee on you. I bought it because I figured, with your early morning flight, you would need some coffee to get through today. And I'm sorry. I didn't mean to kiss you. Um...I'm sorry. I'm not used to the two-cheek-kiss thing you do in Europe. I'm sorry."

I look down at my light-blue shirt and black slacks that are now covered in coffee. It's just not as visible on my pants as it is my shirt. I packed lightly. Everything I brought with me is inside a small carry-on. I doubt that I'm going to be here very long. Jamie just said she needed some help. I'm sure I can have her company headed in the right direction in no time.

"It's fine. I'll just need you to point me in the direction of a dry cleaner later."

"When you get to the office, you can change, and I'll have this dry-cleaned for you by the end of the day."

I nod. "Lead the way."

I follow Olive outside and am thankful that she parked against the curb even though I'm sure it is breaking the rules. You aren't supposed to park your car against the curb.

A security officer is standing outside of Olive's Mercedes.

"Is this your car, miss? It's a no parking zone," the security officer says.

"I'm so sorry. I didn't know. I'll move it right now," Olive says, climbing into the driver's seat.

The officer gives her a stern look but then nods. I toss my carry-on into the backseat and then climb in the front seat, next to Olive. She immediately pulls out and begins driving.

I glance around the interior of her car. It's nice, really nice. "Your car is nice. Jamie must pay you well for you to afford something this nice."

Olive blushes. "It's not my car. It's Jamie's. She gave it to me to come pick you up since I don't own a car."

I look around now, more amazed with Jamie. She's doing well for herself if she can afford this.

"So, what do you do for Jamie?"

"I'm her assistant," Olive answers.

I nod. It makes sense, although I'm not sure Olive is doing the best job she could as an assistant. Maybe that's what Jamie needs me to do. Prune the employees who aren't doing so well to help her continue to grow.

Olive surprises me with how she manages Chicago traffic for someone who doesn't own a car. She drives efficiently and safely but quickly gets us to the office.

"Thanks for picking me up, Olive," I say as I climb out of the car.

"Of course, Sean—I'm sorry. I mean—"

"Don't worry about it. I don't mind if you call me Sean."

She smiles and then leads me into the office building. Then, we ride up in the elevator to the floor that Parks Real Estate occupies.

We climb out, and to my surprise, it seems like the whole team has gathered to welcome me to the building. There are about fifty people gathered with all their eyes focused on me and Olive. I glance over at Olive, who also seems surprised at the gathering.

Olive begins speaking before I have a chance to, "This is Sean—uh, Mr. Sturrows."

She bites her lip when she realizes she said the wrong last name and begins to open her mouth to, I assume, correct herself, but I cut her off.

"I'm Sean Burrows. I'm excited to work with all of you for as long as you and Jamie will have me. I've heard wonderful things about all of you. As for my stained shirt, I've heard that's what happens when you work in real estate and when you have an assistant like Olive pick you up," I joke.

The room chuckles and laughs, obviously used to Olive doing things like spilling coffee on a regular basis, but when I glance over at Olive, I immediately regret my joke. I expected her to look embarrassed or maybe a little upset with my joke. But she doesn't look embarrassed. She looks downright angry.

"I'm so happy you could make it," Jamie says, softly kissing me on the cheek.

"I'm happy to be here. I would do anything for you."

She smiles, and I have a chance to study Jamie. She looks different. Her cheeks look the slightest bit fuller. In fact, her whole body looks slightly fuller. Not in a bad way, but in a perfect way. Her skin seems to be glowing, and her long blonde hair is shinier than I've ever seen it.

I realize immediately why she brought me here, and it's not because she wanted another date or a one-night hook-up or anything to do with me other than she trusts me.

"You're pregnant," I whisper in her ear.

Jamie blushes, and I know it's true.

"Have Olive take your clothes to the dry cleaners and get changed. We have a lot to discuss."

Jamie heads to her office, and I can't help but stare at her gorgeous ass as she walks.

"Come on, Romeo. I'll show you to the restroom, so you can get changed, and I can get your clothes to the dry cleaners. Although no one believes it, I do have more important things to do with my day," Olive says, walking toward the restroom.

I follow her. "Is it that obvious that I like Jamie?"

She shakes her head. "You are unbelievable. How about an *I'm sorry*?"

"Why would I say sorry?"

"Because you said something hurtful at my expense."

"It was a joke. It wasn't hurtful. It was truthful."

"You should apologize instead of worrying if it's obvious that you like Jamie. It's obvious that everyone likes Jamie, so it's not that unusual. No one but me notices because everyone else is already too busy pining over Jamie."

"So, who's the baby daddy?" I ask.

Olive stops and looks at me seriously. "She told you she was pregnant?"

"No, I just guessed. You confirmed."

"I didn't confirm anything."

I smile. "Yes, you did."

"Whatever. Just get changed, so I can take your clothes." She pauses at the restroom for me to go inside. "Although you probably want to take them yourself since I will just ruin them."

I begin unbuttoning my shirt and watch as her eyes drift to my chest and then abs. I remove the shirt and hand it to her. "Just take the shirt. It's a favorite of mine. I'll just buy new pants if I need them."

Olive sucks in a breath and then walks away. I watch her ass sway in her dress. I watch her toned, tan legs move, and then I see that she is still wearing her snow-covered boots. She's adorable and a tiny bit sexy. And a giant mess.

I could have her in my bed as many times as I want while I'm here. Or I could fire her because, if she is this incompetent in how she dresses, she can't be much more competent as an assistant. It's a tough decision—think with my dick or my business sense.

Jamie walks over to me as I pull a shirt out of my suitcase and begin to put it on.

"That wasn't very nice—what you said about Olive," she says.

I roll my eyes. "I was being truthful, and you know it. I don't want to talk about Olive right now. If I do, it will be to suggest firing her. There are a million assistants out there who are better than Olive."

She raises an eyebrow. "Wow. For once, you don't want to fuck my assistant. I thought Olive was just your type."

I laugh. "A complete mess isn't my type."

"Olive is anything but a mess. In fact, she might be the most put-together person in this office."

"So, that's why you pay her so well then?"

"I have my reasons for not paying her as well as I should."

"Yeah. Greed?"

She shakes her head. "Well, I'm glad that you don't want to sleep with Olive."

"Why?"

"Because, as you have already guessed, I brought you here to run the company for me for a few months—a year at most."

"A year? What the hell, Jamie? I can't stay here for a year! I have my own fucking company to worry about."

"Which is doing just fine. And, if I recall, last time we were together, you said the company could run itself."

I frown.

"Anyway, the doctor said I needed to be on bed rest, starting, like, now. I shouldn't even have come into work today. I just wanted you to get settled and to let you know that Olive is the woman you should go to for advice. She's the smartest person at the company. She's more than just an assistant. She is the only person I trust."

"So then, why isn't *she* running the company?"

She sighs. "You'll understand soon enough. You aren't going to fire Olive. Olive is my assistant, and I expect her to still be here when I get back. Plus, she'll be reporting to me about everything that is going on. So, you'd better not fuck up."

"And what if I do fuck up? It's not like it matters anymore. I came here to try to get you back, but you have clearly moved on. What motivation do I have to do the right thing?"

She smiles and moves her lips close to my ear. "Because I know you, Sean Burrows. I know you still love me and will do anything I ask. And I know you've always wanted to own your own real estate company. That's your next venture. I'll make you a fifty-fifty partner after this year."

"It would be easier to just start my own company than do this for a year."

Jamie shrugs and spots Olive out of the corner of her eye. "Maybe. But maybe you wouldn't find something better, something you'd never experienced before."

"And what's that?"

She glances at Olive, and I do, too.

"Real love."

I laugh.

Jamie is crazy. She didn't bring me here to run the company for her, although she definitely needs the help. She didn't bring me here to entice me with an offer to own half of the company. She brought me here to play matchmaker.

She thinks Olive is the woman for me. She couldn't be further from the truth. Olive is a nice girl with what I'm sure is a nice body underneath the bulky clothing. But she is also a complete mess. She apologizes every five seconds and has zero confidence in herself. She's still an assistant. I want a strong woman, like Jamie, who can equal me in bed and in the business world. Not Olive.

"I think you're crazy, Jamie, but you do have one thing right. I love you and will do anything for you."

"So, you'll run the company for the next year in exchange for owning half of it?"

"Yes, but me asking Olive out on a date is not part of the deal. She's an unconfident mess."

Jamie laughs. "Olive is the strongest, most confident woman I know. Who else would have the confidence to wear half of a face of makeup, boots, and no pants in winter? I know I wouldn't."

I laugh. "I guess that's one way to look at it."

2

OLIVE

I hate him.

Sean.

He's an asshole.

I don't know what he's doing here, but he's been in Jamie's office for almost an hour now while I've been sitting outside, at my cubicle, waiting. All I was told was to pick him up from the airport. Jamie didn't tell me anything else. And, even though we are best friends and she tells me everything—including that she found out she was pregnant from her boyfriend of a total of two months—she is often forgetful. I don't think she would remember anything if it wasn't for me.

But, still, I can't stop thinking about how handsome he is. I can't stop thinking about his dark brown eyes, the five o'clock shadow that covers his strong jaw, or how his muscles bulge beneath his clothing.

The door to her office finally opens, and Sean steps out. He walks past me without even glancing at me or anyone else in the office, and he leaves just as quickly as he got here.

"Olive, can you come in here a moment?" Jamie calls out from her office.

I stand up and walk into her office with a large grin on my face, carrying her dry cleaning that she asked me to pick up on my way into the office today.

I've been Jamie's assistant for far too long. Today is the day I have been waiting five years for. Today is the day I'll finally get promoted. There is a management position open, and I know that she wants me in it. That way, when she takes a couple of months off to be with her baby, I can step in and run things for her. She just needs to make it official.

This is the moment when my life changes. This is the moment when I stop being an assistant. I can stop getting coffee or baking cookies. Although I have a feeling, no matter what position I hold in the company, I'll have to keep making cookies. But at least I'll get paid well. At least well enough to afford more than a studio that holds nothing more than a bed and a small couch and something that resembles a kitchen that wouldn't even fit in one of those tiny houses that you see on TV. They should start videoing my life if they want to know what it's like to live tiny.

"You're an angel, Olive," Jamie says standing as I hand over her dry cleaning. "I couldn't very well work today in sweatpants."

I smile as I look down at Jamie's attire to see that she is indeed in sweatpants. I know she has two closets worth of clothes in her apartment, so she should have had something else to wear. Unless she didn't sleep at her apartment last night.

Jamie takes a seat behind her desk and motions for me to do the same.

I take a seat and wait for her to speak, trying to be as polite as I can even though, inside, I'm bursting to say, *Yes, I'll take it!*

Whatever job she is going to offer and whatever level of money that comes with it will be better than what I get paid. I know everyone else in the company makes at least three times as much as I do, and that's being conservative. The best in the company make ten or more times than I do.

"So, I bet you are wondering why I called you in here this morning."

I nod even though I know exactly why she called me in this morning instead of just emailing me a long list of things she needs me to take care of, like she usually does every morning.

"As you know, some things are about to change with how the company is run around here."

I nod again, smiling brightly, as my suspicions seem to be confirmed.

"And, as you know, I'm pregnant. But, at my last checkup, my doctor said I needed to start taking it easy and be on bed rest until the baby is born."

I nod as I look down at her still-flat stomach. There is no way this woman is five months pregnant. I still can't believe it.

"But, anyway, I want to take at least six months off when the baby is born. I want to just be a mom, which means I need to leave someone I trust in charge of the company to ensure it will continue to head in the right direction."

My eyes widen, and my jaw drops a little bit at what she is suggesting. "You think I am capable of doing that?"

Jamie laughs. "Oh, no. I'm sorry. That's not what I meant at all. That would be a huge jump for you, and you are not ready for that at all. But I don't trust my realtors to lead the company either. We both know, if I let that happen, they would just use the leverage to start their own company. No one is loyal like you are to this company."

I smile, but my smile is weak because I have no idea where she is going with this.

"So, anyway, I hired Sean to be me when I'm gone. He's the best, the absolute best. And I just need you to report to me about how things are going while I'm gone and he is in charge. If things aren't going well, I'll end my maternity leave and come back, but if you tell me things are going well, then I will leave him in charge. Can you do that?"

"Of course. Does this new job come with a promotion?"

She laughs again. "I'm so happy you are my assistant, Olive. You always know just what to say to brighten my day. Of course it's not a promotion, just a favor between two friends."

I nod, but I can't keep smiling. I'm not getting promoted. My heart sinks.

I don't understand. Jamie and I have been friends for years. I've been completely loyal to her and the company, but I still haven't earned a promotion. I don't understand, but I'm not going to question her. I trust her completely, and anyway, I owe her.

"Is that all you need?" I ask.

"Yep. I'm still planning on going to your boyfriend's concert tonight. I need one last night out before I'm confined to my bed for these next few months."

I try to smile, but it's impossible to be excited about spending time with my friend tonight. I nod and then leave Jamie's office to try to go about the rest of my day like usual.

I walk back to my cubicle.

"Hey, Olive. Where is the coffee?" Lewis, a realtor in the company, asks as he walks by my desk.

"I'm sorry. I had to go pick up Sean and dry cleaning on my way into the office today. I'll make it soon."

Lewis frowns but walks away, grumbling, "It can't be that hard to make coffee, can it? What are we paying an assistant for anyway if she can't even make coffee?"

I sigh and try to remember that he doesn't mean it. He just hasn't had his morning coffee today, so he's grumpy.

"Olive, where are the cookies for today's open house?" Audrey, another realtor, asks.

"I'm sorry. I was never told you were doing an open house today. I thought it was scheduled for this Saturday."

"It was, but my client moved it late last night. I really need the cookies."

"I'm sorry. I think there are some frozen ones in the fridge that you can warm up and use. They'll taste just as good. I promise." I try to smile to reassure Audrey.

"You really should start making cookies every day. That way, we'll always have cookies. You know clients want us to move things at the last minute all the time."

"I'm sorry. I'll do that in the future. I can go grab you some fresh ones if you want. There is an awesome bakery just around the corner."

Audrey laughs. "I'm sure they are great, but they aren't as good as your cookies are. Your cookies sell houses."

I smile even though, inside, I feel like dying. I like baking cookies. It's a huge stress reliever. But, when I baked a batch of cookies for Jamie's birthday about a year ago, I never thought it would turn into everyone relying on them on a weekly or now daily basis.

I sigh and then get to work. At least, tonight, I'll get to have a little fun, watching Owen, my boyfriend, play his guitar.

———

"When does your ass of a boyfriend go on?" Keri, my friend who used to work at Parks Real Estate with me, asks.

I sigh as I glance at my watch that now reads after eleven p.m. It's going to be another long night with little sleep. "I thought he was already supposed to be on."

I take a sip of the white wine I ordered. It's only my second glass. Though, after the day I had, I am tempted to drink something stronger.

"We are waiting ten more minutes, and then we are leaving," Keri says, sipping on a margarita.

"Oh, relax, and have some fun. Tonight will be the last night I go out in months," Jamie says, sipping on her water.

I frown. "I can't do that to Owen. I promised I would come to his show today."

Keri shakes her head and finishes off her margarita. "You are too good to that boy. You have to be up in less than eight hours. You need to go home and get some sleep."

"Maybe, but I would feel horrible if I missed his show." I take another sip of my wine.

Keri raises an eyebrow. "You wouldn't feel horrible if you broke up with him."

Wine spews out of my mouth. "Why would I break up with him? I love him."

Now, it's Jamie's turn to raise an eyebrow. "Because he treats you like dirt, and you are so much better than him."

"He does not! Just last weekend, he took me to that amazing hotel—"

"And you spent most of your night cleaning up his puke," Jamie says, also ganging up on me.

"He just drank a little too much! It can happen to the best of us."

"It was your birthday, Olive! He was supposed to be taking care of you! Instead, you probably spent the whole night apologizing for letting him drink that much."

I blush. She's right. I did.

"I don't want to talk about Owen anymore." I ask Keri, "How are your classes going?"

She has gone back to school to get an English degree. A degree that I don't have the heart to tell her won't make her more money than what she was making when she was a real estate agent.

"I quit."

My jaw drops open. "What? Really? That's great! There is a new management position open that I think you would be perfect for."

Keri starts laughing until she is snorting.

"What's so funny?"

"I didn't quit. I just wanted to get your honest feelings about if I should be going to school or not, and I knew you wouldn't give me an honest answer unless I told you I'd quit."

"Oh my God! I'm so sorry, Keri! I didn't mean...I mean, you should—"

"Stop apologizing, Olive."

"I'm sorry."

Keri raises an eyebrow at me.

"I'm sorry. I mean—"

Keri shakes her head. "Anything new going on at work?" she asks, looking from me to Jamie.

"I hired someone to be me while I'm gone these next few months," Jamie says.

Keri eyes me but doesn't say anything even though I know she thinks I should be the person for the job.

Jamie turns to me. "What did you think of Sean? You think he'll make a good me while I'm gone?"

I blush. "I'm not the best person to judge Sean. We didn't get off to the greatest of starts."

Keri leans back in her chair, glancing up as Owen and his band finally take the stage. "And why not?"

"Because I didn't make the best first impression with Sean."

"How bad of a first impression?" Keri asks as she studies me with her eyes.

"The kind where I spilled coffee on him, accidentally kissed him on the lips, and introduced him to the team by the wrong name."

Jamie laughs. "You did not! I didn't realize. He usually tells me everything."

I blush a brighter shade of pink.

Keri grins. "Plus, you probably apologized about a million times."

I frown but have to nod.

Owen starts playing with his band, and we all fall silent as we watch him.

An hour later, Keri says, "I need to go home, or I'm never going to get out of bed on time in the morning."

I nod. "Good night."

Keri glances from me to the stage. "Just don't stay all night." She hugs me and then starts walking out of the club. She stops and hollers over her shoulder, "And don't stay up all night, making those asshole real estate agents cookies for their show- ings tomorrow! You need your sleep."

"I won't!" I yell back.

I'll just get up a couple of minutes early and throw some cookies in the oven while I'm getting ready.

I turn my attention back to Owen and his band onstage. At least I have Owen. He might not be perfect, but I love him, and he loves me back. That's enough.

Jamie lays her head on my shoulder. "I'm exhausted. I'm not going to last much longer."

I laugh. "I'll get you into a cab then."

I take Jamie to a cab, and then I go back to my seat to finish watching Owen play. I love watching him play, but I really wish he would book more weekend gigs and less during the week.

I rest my head in hands as I watch him continue to play. I know they still have three or four more songs before they finish their set. I can make it through. I close my eyes. I'll just listen and rest my eyes...

"Olive!" Owen shouts, jolting me awake.

I jump awake.

"I don't know why you even bother coming if you are just going to fall asleep," Owen says.

"I'm sorry. I've had a really long day. Let's just go back to my apartment and go to sleep," I say.

He sighs. "My apartment is so much nicer though. Your apartment is tiny."

"But my apartment is closer to my work, and I haven't seen my cat all day. You don't have to be anywhere in the morning."

He shakes his head. "I'm going to my apartment. You coming?"

I think back to this morning—how late I was going into work because he'd turned my alarm off again, how long of a subway ride it was to get into work.

"I'm sorry. I can't tonight. I'll stay over tomorrow night," I say.

Owen frowns and then leaves without so much as a good-bye kiss.

I love Owen. He loves me, I keep repeating to myself.

We've both just had a bad day today. Tomorrow will be better.

But then I remember that I have to deal with Sean tomorrow, and I realize that tomorrow is going to be just as bad.

3
———

SEAN

IT's eight o'clock sharp when I make my way into Parks Real Estate Office. It's not early by anyone's standards, but considering I own a company that operates mainly in the evenings, it's early for me. I expect to see an office full of life as I walk through the office. Instead, I find a mostly empty office.

What the hell? Does no one come to work on time?

I keep walking toward Jamie's office. I need to take some time to make it mine if I'm going to be working here for a year in Jamie's place. I can only handle so many motivational quotes and hippie incense.

"Good morning, Sean," a sweet voice says as I walk to my new office.

I stop to greet the person when I realize it's Olive. I cock my head to the side as I look at her sitting behind her desk. She looks slightly more put together today than she did yesterday. Her long hair is a little more tamed but still frizzy. She's wearing dark dress pants with dress boots that are much more appropriate for the weather and the office, but somehow, it disappoints me. I quite enjoyed looking at her bare legs yesterday. She looks put together, except when I study her further. Her eyes have the tiniest of bags underneath them. Her lips are stifling the need to yawn. She's exhausted.

"Coming into work early isn't going to win you any favors if you are exhausted and worthless to the team, especially when it's clear that no one comes in this early," I say.

"I'm sorry. I mean..." She shakes off her apology. "I always come in this early. I try to beat Jamie in, so I can make sure the coffee is ready and everything is ready for her. I'm always the first to show up and one of the last to leave. That's who I am. I'm sorry if I seem a bit tired. I had a bit of a long night last night. Tomorrow, I'll be better."

I narrow my eyes at her and resist the urge to laugh at her ridiculous apology. I continue into my office without another word to her.

I begin moving the incense, candles, and pictures of Jamie and her boyfriend off the desk and put them on the floor to make room for my laptop on the desk. I fire it up and open my email. Over a hundred unread messages pop up with more coming in each second as I stare at the computer. Some are from my business, and some are from Jamie's business. Either way, it looks like I'm going to be spending most of my day answering emails.

I really need to find a manager who can be me when I'm not here. I know Jamie doesn't believe in managers, but she doesn't get to complain about how I run the company if she isn't here.

I decide to start with looking through the applicants for the management position that I sent out yesterday. I said that all applications had to be in by noon today, so I expect most everyone who is interested in applying has already applied. Although I'm sure I'll get a few stragglers today. Those who wait until today to send in their applications will get a mark against them. I need people who know what they want and are prepared for anything. Not someone who waits until the last minute.

I pull up the emails that are in reference to the position and am in shock when I see only five applications. Out of more than a hundred employees who work here, only five have applied so far. Hopefully, it's the best five employees.

Did I not make it clear that the position would come with a huge raise?

Everyone should be fighting for the position, not unconcerned about it. Jamie really must have convinced these people that it's better to be happy and have work-life balance than make money because this is not how normal people respond to the opportunity to make a lot more money.

I open the first email. It's from Sandie. She has only one year of experience and is fresh out of college. Not what I'm looking for.

I open the second email from Melissa. Three years' experience. Slightly better but still not what I want.

The third email is from Floyd. Seven years' experience. He claims he brings in more commission than anyone else at the company. And he's male, so he won't distract me from what I need to be focused on. He sounds perfect.

I open the last two emails, and while I know I'll interview all of them, my gut tells me that Floyd is my guy.

The first is more of the same. From Clay, who has limited experience.

The last email almost knocks me on my ass. It's from Olive.

Maybe there is another Olive in the company? One who isn't an incompetent assistant?

But, as I read the email, I know this is the Olive sitting right outside my office. The Olive who spilled coffee on me and apologized for kissing me. That was a first. Most women don't apologize for kissing me. And that was the one thing she did right. If she would just kiss me every time she fucked up instead of apologizing, I would like her a lot more.

I begin reading the email from her.

To Sean Burrows,

I am writing to inform you that I would like to apply for the management position. As an assistant, I know I have limited qualifications, but I am loyal and have been an assistant here for almost five years.

I apologize for the initial meeting where I was late in picking you up from the airport, spilled coffee on you, and introduced you incorrectly, among other things. I know I did not make a great first impression, but I need this job. No one should still be an assistant when entering their thirties.

I have attached my résumé. I'm sorry for taking up so much of your valuable time.

Thank you for your consideration,

Olive Porter

P.S. I'm sorry for kissing you on the lips. I really was trying to kiss you on the cheek. I was told you were European, so I was trying to make you comfortable. I was clearly wrong about both.

I chuckle, reading her email. I don't know why she thinks she should be our manager or why I would even consider her. She has no experience, and on her résumé, she doesn't even list if she has her real estate license. She has no qualifications for the job. But I have to hear her try to explain herself to me. Maybe it will cheer me up from the fact that Jamie will never be mine, but I'm stuck in this frigid, cold place anyway.

I stand up and walk over to my office door before opening it. Olive is seated at her desk, typing away on her computer.

"Olive, I'd like to see you in my office."

She narrows her eyes and frowns but then slowly turns her frown into a fake smile before getting up from her desk. "Of course."

I hold the door open for her as she walks into my office and takes a seat across from me. I take my time in walking back to my seat behind my desk, letting the anxiety that I know she must be feeling creep up higher and higher until I'm sure it's seeping out of every pore in her body.

"Do you know why I called you into my office?"

"No idea," Olive answers honestly.

It's strange not to hear a sir or Mr. Burrows. That's how I'm always treated—formally and with respect. Olive doesn't bother with sir or misters though. At least, she doesn't today.

"I wanted to talk to you about your application."

Her eyes widen. "Is this an interview?"

I smirk at her thinking I would give her an interview so easily. "No, this is more like a preinterview."

"Oh."

"Tell me why you think you have the qualifications to even apply for this position?"

She takes a deep breath, and then for the first time, I see the tiniest spark in her eyes.

"Because I have more experience than anyone other than Jamie in this company. I know my title says assistant, but I do a lot more than a typical assistant would. I am Jamie's right-hand woman. And I know that, if she had to choose a manager, she would choose me. I deserve this position. I've worked my ass off for five years. I've earned a promotion. I don't have my real estate license because it's expensive to take the test, and there was no need to get it if I was never going to get promoted, but I could pass the test in my sleep. I know everything there is to know about real estate, and if I don't get this job, then I quit." She bites her lip when she says the last word, like she didn't mean to reveal to me that she planned on quitting if she didn't get the job.

But her biting her lip has drawn my attention back to her lips instead of staying focused on the task at hand. It would be nice to have that lip on my mouth again.

"You should quit."

Her eyes widen so much, I'm afraid they are going to pop out of her head. "What?"

"If you quit, then I can fuck you, and I really want to fuck you. If you stay, well, then I can't."

God, what am I saying? This is definitely harassment.

I've been forward with women before, but this might be taking it a bit too far. It's just been too long since I've had a woman in my bed.

"I have a boyfriend."

I smirk. "I doubt that."

She frowns. "His name is Owen, and he's a musician. And I quit, but not so that I can fuck you. I quit. Good luck running this company on your own without me. You're going to need it."

I watch as she stands up and begins to walk out of my office. This really isn't going how I planned it.

"Wait," I say, standing up.

To my surprise, she pauses. I don't know why I'm going to say what I'm going to say next. I suspect it's because I'm thinking with my dick instead of my brain. I should just let her walk out of here, but Jamie would be upset with me. And, for the first time today, I've seen something in Olive that I think could be developed into a more confident woman with just a little help. And I know just what she needs to do that. She could become my pet project, and just maybe, I can show Jamie that I'm not such a bad guy. That, if things don't work out between her and her baby daddy, then she should give me a second chance.

"I'll give you a real interview, just like everyone else."

"And you'll stop talking about fucking me and being an asshole in general to me?"

I take a step forward until I'm invading her personal space. "I'll stop talking about fucking you, and I'll try to behave more like your boss instead of an asshole."

"Good. I'll see you for my interview…"

"Tomorrow," I answer.

"Tomorrow. If you need anything taken care of today, let me know. It was nice speaking with you, Sean," she says.

She extends her hand, but she's not paying attention to how close we are, and she grazes across my dick that is hardening more each second.

"I'm so sorry," she says, retracting her hand.

I laugh. She almost made it out of here without apologizing.

"I'll see you tomorrow, Miss Porter."

She turns and walks out of my office without looking back.

I smile to myself as I walk back to my desk chair and picture what it would be like to bend her over my desk and fuck her here. How pink would her cheeks get? Has she ever been fucked properly by a man? Or is she secretly one of those quiet, insecure girls who becomes a fierce tiger in bed?

I promised I wouldn't mention fucking her again, but I didn't promise not to *think* about fucking her.

And that's how I get through the shit-ton of emails I have—by envisioning her naked ass up in the air as I bend her over the desk.

4

OLIVE

I SIT NERVOUSLY at my desk as I watch Floyd enter Sean's office. Floyd is the last person to interview before it's my turn, which means I only have fifteen, maybe twenty minutes tops, until it's my turn to interview. Most of the interviews have taken less time than even that. If I've learned anything from watching Sean interview, it's that he is quick and efficient, most likely because he's already made up his mind of who's going to get the job. If I had to guess who Sean is going to pick, it's going to be Floyd. The other women who applied don't really have the skills for the job or the boobs to make hiring someone with a lack of experience worthwhile.

Floyd is my only real competition. And who am I kidding? I'm no competition for Floyd. The fact that I know more about this company than anyone else other than Jamie doesn't mean I'm qualified for the job. I'm nothing but an assistant. An assistant who's never been promoted and who doesn't have any real responsibilities—at least, not on paper. There's no way that Sean's going to hire me, no freaking way.

I already spent most of my evening looking at the classifieds, trying to find a job that would be a step up and provide me with a lot more opportunities for growth. But, so far, nothing. At least nothing that doesn't require a college degree that I don't have. It means that I will continue being an assistant.

Besides, with all my talk about quitting, I would have a hard time doing that to Jamie. Despite the fact that she's never promoted me, we are good friends, and I know that she's counting on me to make sure that Sean doesn't fuck up her business. I'll stay for the year and maybe take some college classes or something on the side. I'll learn all that I can, and then I'll be better prepared to find a new job when Jamie comes back.

I look down at the blue blouse that I bought to go with the black skirt. I just bought the outfit last night, so I could look my best for this interview for a job that I know I have no chance of getting. I sigh as I undo the top two buttons on my blouse. I know I have no experience and that I have no shot at getting the job. Well, that's not true. My only shot is to look sexy as hell and to convince Sean to give me the promotion because he wants to keep looking at me every day, not because he thinks I'm the most qualified. My only shot is to make him think that he has a chance at sleeping with me even though he has no shot.

I try to focus on answering emails while I wait for my turn to interview. But I can't focus, just like I haven't been able to focus all morning. I shouldn't feel anxious. There's nothing to be worried about. After the interview is over, I'm going to be no better off but also no worse off. Sean already doesn't think well of me, but Jamie will never fire me.

My heart stops when I see the door to Sean's office open. I watch as Floyd exits with a large smile on his face. I glance down at my computer to see the time. Ten minutes. He was in there for ten minutes. That's five minutes less than everyone else's previous interviews. So, if I can keep Sean talking for ten minutes, maybe I'll have a chance. Should be easy, right?

I nod at Floyd as he passes, but he just gives me a smirk and then walks off, like he knows he has the job in the bag. I close my laptop and then take a minute to straighten out my skirt and blouse one last time. I decide to really go for it and unbutton one last button, making sure that my lace bra pokes through just enough beneath the blue blouse.

Then, I stand up. I walk over to his office and knock quietly. "Mr. Burrows, are you ready for me?" I ask, my voice a bit shaky.

"Come in, Olive," Sean says matter-of-factly with no emotion in his voice.

I try to shake off my nerves as I step inside, and I take a seat in the chair across from his desk. The office has changed a lot since Jamie occupied it. Gone are all the girlie candles and paintings, replaced with art that is dark, black, and manly. He doesn't have any picture frames on his desk. Nothing personal at all.

I open my mouth to ask how his day is going, but he speaks first, "What skill sets do you have that you think makes you right for the job?" Sean doesn't look up from his computer.

I blink several times, confused because he's not even really giving me the time of day. But it does make it easier for me to answer him. When he's not looking directly at me, it somehow makes it less intimidating.

"I'm loyal. I think that the most important trait when it comes to being a manager is someone who puts the company first. Someone who cares so deeply about the company that they are willing to give up a part of themselves. They are willing to make sacrifices in order to do more for the team. In real estate, I think it can sometimes get extremely competitive, and I think there needs to be a fair amount of competition in order for individual realtors to do a good job. But we also work for one company, and I think the manager of that company should be one who can inspire and support the team as well as help foster a healthy level of competition."

"And what weaknesses do you have, and how do you plan on overcoming them in this job?" Sean asks, still not looking up from his computer. He clicks on something with his mouse, not paying attention to me.

"You. You're my biggest weakness. Every time your hot-ass body comes in the office, I lose my mind. I can't think about anything else other than you. I struggle to get my work done because all I can do is think about you and how big your cock must be beneath your slacks. And how do I plan to overcome it? By getting you to fuck me a lot," I say because I realize it doesn't really matter what I say. He's not paying any attention to me.

I wait for his next pointless question, but he doesn't ask a question right away, like he did previously. Instead, he slowly closes the laptop sitting in front of him and looks up at me. His eyes travel from mine to my breasts. I glance down and find that I'm exposing a little more of my cleavage than I was planning on.

"What are you doing?" he asks as his eyes travel back up to mine, not bothering to hide the lust that is there after getting a taste of my body.

I fold my arms across my chest. "You aren't taking this interview seriously, so why should I?"

"Maybe because you're the one being interviewed," he says as he leans back in his chair. He cocks his head to the side as he looks at me with an expression I can't read.

"I'll just let myself out and get back to work. Do you want me to let Floyd know that he got the job?" I ask as I stand up.

"Sit down, Olive," Sean commands, like I'm a dog.

"No. I'm tired of being humiliated. I'm sorry if you expect me to quit now, but I'm not. I'm good at this job, and I would have been good at the manager job as well if you had given me a chance. But I promised Jamie that I would stay here as her assistant and keep an eye on you while she was gone. And I'm a woman of my word. So, I'll stay here and report back to her until she returns. Then, I'll find a new job."

I start walking to the door when Sean jumps up, and just as I begin to open it, he slams it shut. I jump back, startled.

"Sit back down, Olive."

Whatever confidence I had a moment ago vanishes when he growls at me that way. The look he is giving me is more than enough to make my panties wet. And I don't even like this man. But the way he's looking at me now is enough to make me forget about all of that.

We cautiously sit back down as we stare intensely at each other.

"What makes you think I'm giving the job to Floyd?"

"Aren't you?" I ask.

"I was, but then you came in here and did that."

My eyes widen. "I don't understand. I just said some ridiculous crap about finding you attractive, and you're going to give me the job because of that?"

He shakes his head. "No. I'm not giving you the job."

"Oh."

"But I am giving you a chance to learn to become a manager. I'll put you through a training program of sorts, and if you pass, then you'll get the job."

"What kind of training program?"

Sean leans forward on his desk as a slow grin spreads on his face. "The kind that's going to test your limits. The kind that will prove to me who the real you is—that confident woman you were just a few minutes ago or the shy, pathetic woman I met the other day. Either way, you're probably going to hate me after this is all over. And there's no way I think you're going to follow through with the program to the end in order to get the job." Sean pauses as he leans back, smiling. "But then again, I've been wrong before."

My mouth drops open in complete shock. I have no idea what Sean is talking about. All I know is that he's giving me a chance to be manager if I complete whatever silly training he has planned. And I'll do anything to make this work.

"Well, I already hate you, so what difference does it make?"

"Is that a yes?" he asks.

"Sorry. Yes, that's a yes."

He shakes his head. "I don't want to hear *sorry* drop from your lips again. That's your first lesson. No more saying *I'm sorry* or apologizing of any sort. Managers don't apologize for the decisions they make. They stand behind them. And, if I hear anything like it again, you will be punished. Do you understand?"

I bite my lip as he says the word *punished*. Because all I can think about are naughty things involving spankings and whips. But I know that's not what he means. It's just my dirty mind playing tricks on me.

"Understood."

"Good. Now, our first real lesson will begin at dinner tonight."

I scrunch my face. "Dinner?"

"Yes, dinner. We both have to eat, and I don't have time to train you during normal work hours. I have enough on my plate with running my own business and keeping Jamie's afloat while she's gone. I need a manager to get on board as fast as possible to help me out when I need to travel for my own business."

I nod. "I understand that, and I'm willing to come in after hours or do whatever it takes to get this job. It's just that I was unaware that training was going to start tonight, and...well..."

"For goodness' sake, spit it out, Olive!"

"It's my and Owen's one-year anniversary tonight. We were going to go out to dinner."

"The training times and places are nonnegotiable. I don't

want to hear your excuses or reasons for not being able to attend them. Either meet me for dinner tonight or consider yourself out of the running for the job, and I'll just give it to Floyd. It will make both our lives easier. You can go out with Owen or whatever after we finish our training. I don't care if you starve and wait and eat until after we're done, most likely nine thirty or ten, but I will be eating."

I frown, trying to think about what I should do. I think about what Keri would say. That I should go out with Sean. Do something for me for once. Give myself a shot at taking my career to the next level. Owen and I can always go out tomorrow night to celebrate our anniversary.

"What time and where do you want me to meet you for dinner?" I ask.

Just the tiniest bit of a grin forms on his face. "Seven. And we can leave from here. I'm sure you have more than enough work to get caught up on 'til then since I know you got nothing done this morning," he says with a smirk.

I frown and storm out of his office before he can say anything more to me. I have to cancel my date with Owen, but I have a chance at a job that could change everything for me. Absolutely everything.

As I walk back to my desk, I see the men in the office staring at my chest, and I quickly button up my blouse. I have a chance at the job I want, but somehow, I'm worried that it's going to feel more like a date than training. I shake my head.

Jamie would be proud of me for what just happened. She always says I need to use everything I have to go after what I want. Not just my head, but my body, too. It turns out that maybe she was right. That my body and dirty mouth might actually come in handy. They might actually get me the promotion. I just hope I'm not biting off more than I can chew when it comes to Sean.

5

SEAN

What the hell am I doing?

That's the question that keeps running through my head as I try to answer the dozens of emails that fill my inbox. I've hardly gotten anything done this afternoon since Olive's interview.

I had no intention of turning Olive into a manager. I don't even know if it's possible to turn her into a competent manager. She's a complete mess. She has zero confidence in herself, which makes me have zero confidence in her ability to manage people. And, to make matters worse, she doesn't even have her realtor's license.

But the way she acted when she entered my office changed everything. She had me entranced from the second she spoke. She brought me further under her spell when I looked up and saw how provocatively she was dressed. I usually hate women who dress so provocatively to try to get ahead in the world, but it's a proven fact that it works. And I had no idea that Olive had it in her to pull such a dirty trick like that. But, evidently, there's a hint of a strong, fierce woman beneath her weak exterior. Maybe, just maybe, I can find a way to keep that strong, fierce woman on the surface.

But there's another reason I asked her to dinner tonight. Because I want her all to myself. After seeing her in my office, I want her more than I've ever wanted anything. Even money.

I glance at my watch. I still have thirty minutes until I told her to be ready to go to dinner. But I can't wait any longer, and I'm not getting any useful work done anyway. I close my laptop and roll my sleeves down before I walk over and grab my coat off the coat rack in the corner of the room. Then, I walk out of Jamie's office and find Olive sitting at her desk.

She immediately spots me, like she has been staring at my door, waiting for me to come out, but when I catch her gaze, and she realizes she has been caught, she begins clicking furiously on her mouse while burying her head behind the computer screen, trying to act like she has been working this whole time. But I know that she hasn't gotten any more work done than I have.

I know that I affect her. As much as she tries to deny it and pretend like she has a boyfriend, I know that she wants me as badly as I want her. And, despite how wrong it might be to fuck my assistant, who has led me to believe she could be a manager, I don't care. I've done much worse in the past.

"I hope you got all your work done, Olive, because I finished early, and I'm ready to go to dinner now."

She nods and then fidgets with her computer a second more before closing it. I examine every inch of her body as she closes her laptop. I notice that her shirt is buttoned much higher than it was in my office, much to my disappointment. Although I'm happy that the rest of the men in this office didn't get the same show that I did.

I shake my head. *Where did that come from?* I can't be jealous of other men looking at Olive.

I watch as Olive puts her computer into a backpack. I sigh but don't say anything. She then walks over and grabs the same bright, puffy pink coat that she wore to pick me up from the airport. I grab it out of her hand and then walk over and drop it in the trash.

"Hey! That was my coat! What are you doing? I can't go outside without a coat. It's freezing."

"You can wear mine," I say, shrugging mine off and handing it to her.

She frowns as she takes my coat from me. "What's wrong with my coat?"

"If you have to ask, you'll never understand what's wrong with your coat."

"You owe me a new coat."

"Fine. I'll have my assistant send a new coat to your place in the morning."

"Aren't I your assistant? So, doesn't that mean I will be buying myself a coat?" she asks.

I sigh. "You aren't my only assistant, Olive."

She frowns. "But I like my puffy coat. I don't need a new coat."

I frown. "If you want the manager job, you're going to have to start dressing like a manager, and that means, no puffy coats."

"Fine," she says, rolling her eyes.

I start walking toward the elevator, resisting the urge to grab her hand because I know it would be inappropriate. But I do manage to place my hand on the small of her back as I lead her into the elevator. I do get close enough to smell the pretty apples and cherry scent oozing off her frizzy hair. I need to remember to get her a salon appointment. I know that alone would do wonders for her confidence even though I do like her untamed hair a bit.

"Should I get an Uber?" Olive asks as we ride down in the elevator.

"No."

"No?" Olive asks, cocking her head to the side to look at me.

"I leased a car since I'm going to be here for months."

"Oh."

The doors open, and I can't handle it anymore. I grab her hand and pull her hard out of the elevator. "Come on," I say impatiently, giving her a reason for why I am holding her hand that has nothing to do with how badly I need to touch her.

I lead her down the hallway and out to the parking garage where my Audi S4 is parked. I reach into my pocket and pull out my keys to unlock the car. I walk her to the passenger side and open the door without thinking.

Olive looks up at me, wide-eyed, as I help her into my car. I try to look annoyed, like the reason for me helping her is because I don't think she is capable of quickly getting into the car by herself. Her wide-eyed expression quickly turns into an annoyed frown.

I smirk as I run around to the driver's side. She really doesn't think that I'm into her at all. And I'm going to keep it that way. If she thinks I want her, then I'm giving up some of the control to her. And I hate doing that. I'd rather her come to me. I want her begging, willing to do anything, because she needs me so badly. And, until she gets to that point, I'll keep my hands off of her.

I drive quickly out of the parking spot. The tires squeak against the pavement as I turn too fast around the corner of the parking garage. Olive sucks in a breath and grabs hold of the door handle. Her eyes stay open wide as I whip out onto the street. But she doesn't ask me to slow down. She doesn't say anything. It's like, in the last couple of hours since her interview, she has reverted back to the unconfident, quiet woman she was before.

I smirk. We will see how long she can last without getting that confident, sassy mouth back. I press my foot down harder on the gas. We speed up, flying past cars at a speed that I know is far past her comfort level.

She still doesn't say anything though. Instead, her grasp on the door handle gets tighter. She squeezes her eyes shut as I speed up faster to zip around another car, barely squeezing in front of the car as I switch lanes.

I frown, determined to break her. I slow down, pausing at a stoplight, allowing her to catch her breath for just a second. Her eyes slowly open, and her grip on the door handle loosens.

"Have you been to Alinea before?" I ask.

Olive looks at me with wide eyes, but I can't keep my eyes focused on hers. Instead, I move them to her chest that is rising and falling hard as she breathes heavily, giving me a great view of her breasts as they poke in and out of the blouse she is wearing.

"No. Is that where we are going? That place is really expensive," Olive says.

I grin. "Good thing I make a lot of money then," I say as the light turns green.

I whip around the corner, and she tries to grab hold of the door handle again, but I caught her off guard, so she can't. I can feel the panic oozing off her body as I drive.

Still, I keep driving faster. Not because I love it—although I do like driving fast, like any other warm-blooded male does—but because I need her to tell me to stop. I never drive this fast, preferring instead to drive safe and planned, like everything else in my life, but I'm more than willing to change all of my plans when it comes to Olive.

"Stop!" Olive screams as I accelerate again, getting far too close for her comfort to the car in front of us.

I slam on the brakes, immediately slowing us down to a more reasonable speed.

I glance over at her panicked expression on her face.

"What are you doing? Trying to get us killed?"

I frown. "No. Just trying to get you to actually speak up for yourself with some confidence."

She glares at me. "You did this on purpose to try to get me to yell at you? You could have killed us!"

"You should have told me to stop."

She runs her hand through her hair, her hand shaking a little as it combs through her long strands. "I was trying to be nice. This is your car. I don't like telling people how to drive or what to do."

My frown deepens, and my grip on the steering wheel tightens. "Then, why did you apply for the manager job? All it is, is telling people what to do."

She opens her mouth and then quickly closes it again. "I meant, in my personal life."

I shake my head as I pull over in front of the restaurant. "You don't get a personal life. If you are going to keep working for me, everything is about business."

The valet opens her door, and I open my own. I step out before walking around to her side of the car to wait for her. I flip the valet the keys and resist the urge to hold my arm out to her. I take a step forward, but Olive is no longer by my side.

"You coming?" I ask.

Olive scurries forward and then whispers in my ear, "I think we should go somewhere else. This place is really nice, and I'm not really dressed that nicely."

I look up and down her body that is covered in my coat as she wraps it even tighter around her body.

"I'm wearing slacks and a button-down shirt. Do you think I'm dressed nicely enough for this restaurant?"

She pauses a second, studying my clothing. "Yes. You look great. I mean, hot. I mean..."

I grin when she says I look hot. "And why do you think I'm dressed nicely enough to eat at this restaurant?"

She studies me a minute and then shrugs.

I sigh. "Because of the way I carry myself. I don't give anyone the option to even think that I don't belong in here. I'm going to eat here because it is one of the best restaurants in the city. I like splurging on the finer things in life. And I'm freezing my butt off. You can join me or not."

I turn and walk inside, hoping to God that she follows me because, more than anything, I want to torture this woman all through dinner. And then I want to torture her in my bed.

6

OLIVE

I SURVIVED the death trap that was the car ride over here, only to learn it was a test. A stupid test. And it all could have ended if I had just said stop.

That's how Sean is going to play it. He's going to throw test after test at me and hope that I give up and quit. This is all just a fun game to him.

A game he isn't going to win.

Now that I know his game, he no longer has the upper hand. I'm prepared for anything now.

I'm just not prepared for the stares as I walk into the most expensive restaurant that I have ever walked into. I'm wearing the dressiest clothes I own, but it still doesn't feel like enough to be inside this restaurant.

"Can I take your coat?" a man asks as soon as I enter the restaurant.

I nod even though I don't want to give up my coat. I want to keep wearing it because it hides the fact that my outfit isn't enough. It's far too cheap, and it shows the second that Sean's coat is gone.

Sean continues walking once inside, like he owns the place. Maybe he does.

I follow but immediately feel everyone's eyes go from Sean to me as we walk through the restaurant. When they look at him, they are in awe. When they look at me though, they are wondering why I'm with a guy like him. Even in slacks, he looks like he belongs while I look like...an assistant.

I sigh.

We finally make it to our table, a small circular one near the window that looks out at the city. We take a seat across from each other. I smile, trying to act like walking through the restaurant and getting stared at didn't bother me.

Sean smirks, and I know that he knows how uncomfortable I was while walking in here.

The waiter comes over and looks at Sean. "Mr. Burrows, so nice to see you again. Would you like your usual?"

Sean nods.

The waiter then looks at me, a bit surprised. "And what can I get you? Or do you need a few moments with the menu? I can start you off with something to drink."

I know I need to make a decision quickly. That is what Sean wants. A decisive woman who is willing to stand up for herself.

I glance at the wine menu in front of me. "I'll have your house pinot grigio and..." I glance down at the menu and find the cheapest thing I can find. "The Caesar salad."

The waiter raises an eyebrow and then looks at Sean, like he is going to approve or deny what I just ordered. Sean and him exchange some kind of secret conversation that I'm not privy to.

"Very good, sir," the waiter says.

"What was that about?" I ask after the waiter has left.

"You come to the best restaurant in town, and that is what you order? A salad and cheap wine?"

I frown and then lean back as waiters begin pouring us water, and a napkin is placed in my lap.

"You know what my salary is. I can't afford anything more."

He chuckles. "You think I would let you pay?"

I feel the anger growing fast inside me. "Excuse me? Let me pay? I'm more than capable of paying for my own dinner, thank you." I throw my napkin down on the table, not caring that I am making a scene. "You know what? This job isn't worth it."

Sean stands and grabs my hand. "Stay. I'm just trying to push your buttons. It seems it's the only way to get that fierce, sassy mouth to tell me how you really feel."

I frown. "You can push me without insulting me."

He nods and slowly sits back down while I still stand, towering over him.

"I would love for you to have dinner with me. I'll try my best to behave."

He grins, and everything inside me calms. One stupid grin, and I believe everything he says. I slowly sit back down.

An appetizer platter larger than anything I have ever seen and a bottle of wine are brought out. My eyes grow large as I watch Sean taste the wine and then nod in approval. I can't believe the amount of food that has been placed in front of us, and this is just the appetizer. The waiter pours me the red wine as well and then leaves us in peace.

"I don't like red wine," I say, looking at the full glass in front of me.

"You'll like this one."

I frown. "I doubt it."

"Just try it," he says, sighing.

I take a sip and immediately say, "I don't like it."

But it's a lie. I've never tasted anything so smooth, sweet, and delicious as this glass of wine.

He raises an eyebrow.

"Fine. It's delicious. Why do you have to be right all the time?"

He smirks. "I like being right. So, you'd better get used to it."

"So, Mr. Right, what do you recommend I try from this appetizer platter since there is no way I'll be able to eat it all along with whatever you ordered me for dinner?"

He laughs and then says, "Try the squash blossoms. But I would try to make room for a bite of everything."

I sigh and take a bite of one of the squash blossoms. I close my eyes as the food swirls around my taste buds before I finally swallow. When I look up, I see Sean smiling at me.

"What?" I ask.

He shakes his head. "Do you know that you moan when you eat?"

"I do not."

He laughs. "You just did."

"Well, that is because this food is delicious."

I take another bite and try not to moan, but I can't help it. The food is the most delicious thing I have ever eaten. I keep my eyes open this time while I eat, staring intently into Sean's eyes. He swallows hard, like he is struggling with something as he watches me eat, but I can't imagine a man like Sean struggling with anything.

I take a sip of the wine, and I watch his gaze shift from my mouth to my throat as the liquid goes down. It's almost like...I'm turning him on. But that can't be. He doesn't find me attractive. I've messed up too many times for him to find me the least bit attractive. And it would be entirely inappropriate for anything to happen between us. He's my boss.

But the way he is looking at me tells me something different. It tells me he wants me. And the way my heart is beating in return tells me something that I thought was impossible to feel. That I want him, too. Strictly in a sexual way. After all, from what I can tell with his clothes on, his body is all muscle. I'd love to see what is beneath his clothes.

I have a boyfriend though, whom I love deeply. I'm not going to throw a year away just so I can see what my boss looks like naked. I have to stop whatever is going on between us. Now.

"So, should we talk business since that is why I am here? What would you like to discuss?" I ask.

Sean smirks. "We don't need to talk business. It would be a waste until I'm confident you have the skill set to be a leader. I don't really think understanding how the company works is your problem. I'll pay for you to take the realtor's test, and I'm sure you'll pass with no problem. Once you have the leadership skills, then we can talk business. That is the easy part to teach."

I take another bite of food. "Then, why am I here? I thought you brought me here to train me."

"I did."

I blink rapidly. "I'm confused."

"Eat, and then I'll give you your first lesson," Sean commands.

And so, we do. We eat mostly in silence, just enjoying our food. We don't have to say much to each other because the food more than makes up for entertainment. It is the most delicious meal I have ever eaten. But, as our dinner comes to an end, I grow more and more anxious, trying to figure out what his plan is.

The waiter brings Sean the check, and I try my best not to snoop and find out how much this extravagant meal cost. But Sean doesn't even glance at the number. He just throws his credit card down on the bill, like it's nothing. I need to spend some time researching him later to understand what he does when he's not driving me crazy. Then, maybe we can be on a level playing field.

"So, what is this training you have planned?" I ask.

Sean shakes his head. "You're impatient, aren't you, Olive?"

I frown. "No. Just curious."

The waiter returns with the bill.

Sean signs the receipt and then gets up. "Follow me," he says.

I stand and follow him, but we don't go far. Just to the bar. Sean takes a seat in the booth, and I take a seat opposite him, more confused than ever.

"Relax, Olive. You are going to have to learn to trust me if you are going to work for me."

"I work for Jamie. She was the one who hired me. You're just a temp."

Sean sighs as he runs his hand through his hair. He glances over at the bar. I assume he's found a hot woman to take home for tonight.

"Lesson number one: Confidence. That is the number one thing you need to be a leader. Get that guy over there to buy you a drink."

"What?"

"If you can get that guy to buy you a drink, then you can convince someone to buy a house or an employee to change how they work."

"I have a boyfriend though."

Sean laughs. "I'm not asking you to date the guy. Just get him to buy you a drink. If you can do that in a place like this, then I must have really underestimated you."

I narrow my eyes. He doesn't think I can do this.

"Fine." I get up and look at the man Sean is looking at.

He's dressed in a suit, sitting at the bar by himself. He's about my age, but far more successful, it seems. He's good-looking. Not as good-looking as Sean, but he's still way out of my league.

He doesn't know that though. All the man knows is that I ate at this restaurant, same as him. And, as long as he doesn't know much about fashion, then he won't know that my whole outfit cost less than thirty dollars and that I got it from a thrift store.

I start walking toward him, trying to be as confident as I can, when I hear Sean say, "I would unbutton that top button or two if I were you. That's what got me."

I feel my body fuming. But then I remember everything else Sean has done today. Every time was to get a reaction out of me. Every time was to build that fire up inside me. Well, it worked. I'm fired up, but I'm just not sure I can handle any more of Sean's *training*.

I have to find a way to prove to him that I can be a strong, confident woman who is perfect for the job. I'm not sure how to convince him, but I'll start with getting this guy to buy me a drink without unbuttoning my shirt.

I slide onto one of the high-top chairs next to him. Even though there are dozens open, I've chosen the one right next to him.

The man looks over at me.

"I'm Olive," I say with a large smile on my face.

"I'm Dave. And, as much as I would love to sit next to you while we both enjoy a drink, my wife is going to be here any second and would love to sit next to me. So, if you don't mind scooting down a couple of seats, that would be great."

I nod and bite my lip as I make my way back over to where Sean is sitting.

He laughs. "Failed already?"

"He's married and meeting his wife here. I don't think that was really a fair fight."

He shrugs. "It wouldn't stop most married men."

I frown while he laughs at me again.

"Okay, fine, fine. You can try again." Sean glances around the bar and then spots the next target. He nods toward the guy who must have just sat down at the bar. "Get him to buy you a drink."

I smile. "Done," I say, getting back up and walking over to the man seated at the bar.

Of all of the men Sean could have picked, he picked the one I know I will be able to get to buy me a drink. I'm almost to him when a blonde woman takes a seat next to him.

I frown. She isn't going to get him because the man she is flirting with is already taken. By *me*.

The woman grabs hold of his neck and begins kissing him. He doesn't fight her off. He kisses her back.

I freeze.

I never thought I would be in this situation, but here I am.

It doesn't take me long to decide what to do. I finish walking toward him and tap him on the shoulder. Slowly, Owen, my boyfriend, soon-to-be ex, turns around and looks at me with wide eyes.

"Olive. Hi, baby! Uh...this isn't what it looks like," Owen says.

I slap him hard across the cheek. "We are through, Owen."

I turn back and walk toward Sean, angrier than I have ever been. Owen wasn't perfect; I knew that. But I loved him, and he loved me—or so I thought. Now, that's gone.

I look over at Sean, who now has a large grin on his face. I know I'm about to do something else I never thought I would do. I'm going to fuck my boss.

7

SEAN

Olive slapped the guy. My eyes are so wide that they are practically popping out of my head as I stare at her. I can't believe that she is the same woman who wouldn't even tell me to slow down when I was driving at reckless speeds. This woman has two very different sides to her personality. I just can't figure out which one is the real her.

She hasn't even slapped me yet, and she hates me. So, whatever this guy did must have been really bad. Or she thought that it would impress me since she couldn't get the guy to buy her a drink.

Olive stares at me as she walks back to our table.

"What was that?" I ask.

"Can we go?" Olive asks.

I raise an eyebrow. "Is that a question or statement?"

She sighs. "I don't have time for your tests or training or whatever this is right now. I want to go. Now."

I nod and get up from the booth, but she doesn't immediately storm out. Instead, she freezes. I put my hand on the small of her back because, honestly, it looks like she needs me to guide her out of the restaurant and keep her standing.

When we finally get to the front of the restaurant, the hostess goes and gets my coat. I take it from her and help Olive into it. She puts it on, but it's almost like she's a zombie. Her eyes are blank, and she's just going through the motions. She's not really here with me.

I guide her outside where the valet, thankfully, already has my car waiting. The valet opens the door, and I help her into the car before going around to the driver's side. But I don't immediately start driving off. I need answers. Now.

"What happened back there?" I ask.

"Did you see what happened with the guy at the bar?" Olive asks.

I nod.

Of course I watched her at the bar. I'd set up this test for her, hoping that seeing her hit on another man would make me stop wanting to fuck her. But it backfired on me. Seeing her attempt to pick up another man drove me even wilder with need. My whole body grew furious at the sight of her anywhere near another man. Because I want her for myself. I don't want to share.

"Well, the guy sucking face with the blonde was Owen, my boyfriend."

My eyes widen. The boyfriend was real. I truly thought it was something she'd made up.

"Well, ex-boyfriend now anyway." She looks up at me, cocking her head to one side as she studies me. "I guess you aren't going to tell me that you're sorry."

"Would it help?"

"No, it wouldn't."

"Then, why would I waste words by saying something that'd never make you feel any better?"

She nods in agreement. "I guess I didn't pass your test since I didn't get a guy to buy me a drink."

"I would say you passed the first lesson with flying colors."

She raises an eyebrow at me.

"You slapped a guy in the nicest restaurant in all of Chicago. I would say you showed that you have more than enough balls to be a leader. Now, you just have to learn to be that person on a regular basis."

She laughs. "So...your place or mine?" she asks.

I choke on nothing. *Did she just say that?*

Of all the ways I saw tonight ending, this wasn't it. Sure, I hoped in my own twisted way, but I didn't think it would actually happen.

She bites her lip, trying to keep her grin at bay. She's not blushing or showing any signs that she's embarrassed by what she said. She meant every damn word.

"Are you sure you want me to fuck you? He won't take you back after this, if that's a concern of yours. I'm not sure you're ready for the severe consequences of saying yes," I say, reminding her of the boyfriend—or ex-boyfriend.

"I'm not taking him back after this. And why are you asking me if I'm sure anyway? I thought you would say something about how managers always make a decision, and once that decision is made, they don't go back on that decision. Managers just deal with the consequences, so be sure of your decision before saying anything."

I smirk. "That does sound like me. But that was a lesson I was saving for later."

She takes a deep breath and then exhales slowly while she thinks for a moment and then another.

She's going to say no. She's going to come to her senses and realize that fucking me is not going to solve any of her problems. It's just going to create new ones. New problems that involve a complicated relationship where she fucked her boss and would have to come into the office tomorrow and every day after, wondering if the reason she got promoted, was getting special attention, was yelled at, or fired was because she'd fucked me.

And, as much as I know that the sensible thing to do is for her to say no, I'm begging her to say yes. Not to mention, my own experience. I know better than to fuck an employee. Jamie might have been the worst mistake of my life. I ended up losing the only woman I ever cared about.

"Your place or mine?" Olive asks again, more slowly this time.

I grin. "Mine."

———

"Holy crap!" Olive says when I open the door to my condo.

I smirk as I hold the door open for her. "Are you going to go inside?" I ask.

Olive tears her eyes away from my condo and looks up at me. "Please tell me this isn't your condo. Tell me that you have some rich friend you're staying with or that this is your parents' place."

I chuckle and rub the back of my neck, feeling weird for the first time ever about how nice of a place I have. I've never cared what a woman thought, and I for sure have never felt ashamed to have a place this nice, but the way that Olive is looking at me right now makes me feel like maybe I should be ashamed.

"It's not mine."

"Thank God," Olive says, exhaling.

She finally steps inside my condo while I walk in behind her, enjoying the view as I stare at her tight ass in the tight black skirt she's wearing.

"Technically, it's not mine."

Olive flips her head around and looks at me. "What?"

I smile, loving throwing her off her game. "Technically, it's not mine because I'm just leasing it for the year. I'll decide after that if I want to buy the property or not."

Olive's mouth drops open, and then she slowly looks around my condo—up at the ceiling that's two stories tall and around the large room that contains everything, except my bedroom and bathroom. Her eyes go over the kitchen that is full of stainless steel and granite, then across the dark hardwood floor to my living room where all the furniture is pointed at the floor-to-ceiling windows that look out over the city, and then over to the dining room that can easily seat twelve beneath a large chandelier.

"Where's your TV?" she asks.

I walk up behind her and inch as close as I dare without touching her. Close enough that I can smell her and feel every emotion oozing off her body. Nervousness. Anger. Excitement. Need for sex.

"Why would I need a TV for entertainment when I can have this?" I reach out my hand and gently caress her neck, turning her toward me before I press my lips against hers.

Her whole body shivers at my touch, which only makes me want to kiss her more. Deeper. So, I do, and when I finally pull away, all I see are her gorgeous, big eyes staring at me.

I smile weakly. I know she's not ready to throw her whole life away, which is what she would be doing if she fucked me. I'm not boyfriend material, and Olive is the kind of girl who needs a boyfriend. She's not ready. Not yet. Not without some liquid courage at least, and even that I'm sure won't be strong enough to convince her that she wants me to fuck her tonight.

I know women like her. They want commitment, a relationship. They want to be wined and dined first before they fuck. It's best I stay clear of women like Olive because I would destroy them.

"Can I get you something to drink?" I ask as I start heading for the bar my kitchen.

Olive doesn't say anything. She just follows me as her eyes continue to look around my condo. When I get to the bar, I pull out a bottle of wine similar to the one that she drank at dinner. I uncork the bottle and then pour us each a glass since I doubt she's going to tell me her drinking preference when she can barely speak at the moment. I slide the glass over to her where she's leaning against the counter, still staring up at the ceiling that feels small to me compared to my place in Las Vegas, although it's comparable to my place in New York.

"What do you do to make all this money?" are the words she finally says when she opens her mouth. Not, *How dare you kiss me*, or something along those lines. She just continues her thoughts, as if the kiss never happened.

I narrow my eyes as I take a sip of my wine, trying to understand this woman. I slowly set the glass back down. "You're not ready to know what I do yet."

She pouts. "What's that supposed to mean? How could I not be ready to find out what another person does for a living?" She pauses a second and then says, "Unless it's because you do something illegal. Are you in the mob? Do you kill people for a living?" Olive says, taking a step back.

"You'll find out soon enough."

Her eyes widen, and her soft pink lips fall apart. "You expect me to fuck you without even knowing what you do for a living?"

I sigh. "I don't think you're really going to let me fuck you."

"Then, why am I here?"

I lean forward, inching closer to her, while trying to convince myself to stay back. That this isn't actually happening and to not get too excited. "Because you're scared. Scared because the only guy you ever loved cheated on you, broke your heart, and you're trying to find some answers to make yourself feel better. You think sex with me is that answer, but you'll never really go through with it—at least, not until you drink a bottle or two of wine first. But, if you do that, I'm not going to fuck you anyway. I don't have sex with women who are that out of it."

"Well, I'm sorry, but you're wrong because the only thing I'm certain about tonight is that you're going to fuck me," she says. She glances down at her wine. "And I'm sorry you're wasting your expensive wine on me because I don't want any of it. I want you to fuck me, make me forget about my ass of a boyfriend, whom I spent an entire year with."

I grin.

"What?" she asks slowly as she looks at me.

"I told you what would happen if you said sorry in front of me. I told you that you'd be punished. And I'm a man of my word."

8

OLIVE

PUNISH ME.

Those words keep running through my head as a look on Sean's face gets more and more serious. I've been trying with everything in my power to remind myself not to say *I'm sorry* since the moment he told me that he would punish me if I did. But all it took was a little bit of distraction, and now, I'm right back into slipping into my old habits. And I'm terrified to find out what kind of punishment he has in mind. I always assumed that the punishment would be sexual in nature. From the look on his face now, I know that it is.

"You're not seriously going to punish me because I apologized for not drinking what I know is a very expensive wine, are you?" I ask.

Please, God, let him be joking.

I want him to fuck me. I want to feel what it's like to be with a man with experience, who knows exactly what he's doing with my body, but I'm not sure I'm ready for any sort of pain first. I've never done anything the least bit adventurous when it comes to sex, but I know I don't like pain. I didn't even like getting my ears pierced.

"I'm going to punish you, Olive, because it's the only way for you to learn your lesson. But you're lucky this time because I think you're going to enjoy it, too."

I open my mouth to speak, trying to come up with something to say to keep him from punishing me. But, before I get a chance to say anything more, his lips claim mine. This kiss is different than the first. This time, he devours me without any hesitation. Last time was a test. This time, he doesn't ask for permission to kiss me. He demands it. And, through his kiss, I forget about any promises of punishment because any level of pain would be worth this kind of pleasure.

He suddenly breaks the kiss, and I gasp like I need him as much as I need air. He grabs hold of my hand and starts pulling me down the hallway on his left.

"I want to show you the reason I'm leasing this place. I like the openness of the main room for guests and parties." He pulls me further down a long hallway to a door at the end. He stops while he grabs hold of the door and looks at me with a mischievous grin. He turns the knob and pushes the door open. "But this is why I love this condo."

I gasp when I see the dark room. It looks like a dungeon and is so different than the bright openness of the rest of his condo.

"What is that?" I ask even though I clearly know what it is. His bedroom and torture chamber.

He chuckles. "My bedroom. What did you think it was?"

I warily look at him, and he laughs again. He puts a finger under my chin, lifting my gaze to his, before he tenderly kisses me on the lips.

"Relax, Olive. It's just a man's bedroom. I don't have whips hanging on the walls. I don't have handcuffs hiding in drawers. Just a dark, manly room where I can retreat to when I need a break from the world."

I exhale deeply, not realizing that I was holding my breath the whole time.

"Oh, and I also like it because it's soundproof."

And, just like that, he takes my breath away again.

"Now, for that punishment. Since this might be the only time I get to punish you in any sort of sexual manner, I'm going to take full advantage."

"Just no whips or bondage," I whisper loud enough for him to hear.

He laughs. He walks over and softly kisses me on the lips again. "You weren't listening. I already told you, I don't have any whips or bondage in this bedroom. I've used it in the past, and I will again if that's what you really want, but I prefer to use other means to punish and control."

I cock my head to the side as I look up at him, confused. "Control?"

He nods. "That is going to be your punishment. For your lesson tonight, you're gonna learn what it's like to not have any control and therefore learn that you never want to give it up again."

It doesn't sound like that bad of a punishment since it's not like I would know what to do in the bedroom with a man like Sean anyway.

"Why does everything have to be a lesson with you? Why can't we just get back at Owen for breaking my heart, and that's it?"

"Because what fun would that be? And, besides, our time together is limited. I need to take advantage of every second we are together to teach you everything I know."

He doesn't have to say that he thinks our time is numbered because, after tonight, I might give up and quit. He thinks I can't handle working for a man who fucked me and then wanted nothing to do with me. But he doesn't know me at all. He doesn't know how loyal and determined I can be to do something when I've set my mind to it.

"Do we have an arrangement then? Will you give up control and do whatever I say? Let me fuck you however I want?"

I stare into Sean's eyes as my heart races in my chest. I've had sex with a total of three men in my life. None of them were amazing in bed. All were pretty selfish, more worried about their own pleasure than mine. And I have a feeling that's what Sean's about, too. But I know he'll have a different intensity than the rest, and that intensity will at least make me forget about Owen and what he did to me. I want to know what it's like to be fucked by a real man. And, if I have to give up some control to get it, so be it. I can always back out in a moment anyway. All I have to do is say no, and he'll stop. I know that much about Sean. This is him just trying to prepare me for whatever test he has up his sleeve now.

"Yes."

As soon as I say the word *yes*, the door slams shut, making me jump. I'm trapped. Saying no isn't going to get me out of this. I'm not even sure I would have the strength to say no anyway.

"I think I'm going to enjoy this a little too much," Sean says as he walks toward me.

I don't move. I can't move. There's too much excitement and fear running through my veins for me to be able to think clearly enough to do something as simple as move.

He walks forward until his lips are hovering over mine. He looks me in the eyes one more time, challenging me to stop this, giving me one last chance before I completely relinquish all my control to him. It's just a second, but it feels like forever while I wait for him to kiss me.

He doesn't wait for words this time. He just kisses me. I can't breathe, and I'm not sure I want to ever again because all I want to feel is his tongue on mine, pushing further into my mouth, claiming every inch of my mouth as his.

I never thought a kiss could tell me so much, but his kisses tell me everything he's feeling. How his lips press firmly against mine and how his tongue pushes inside me—it shows me how much he wants to fuck me. His hands holding firm on my neck and my ass show me how much control he has over me.

He lets go of me, breaking the kiss, and then says, "Breathe, Olive."

I do, but I don't take a deep enough breath before his lips cover mine again, making me forget all about the fact that I'm not getting enough oxygen. He pushes the kiss right to my limit, knowing full well that I won't breathe again until his lips leave mine—not because I can't, but because I'm completely under his spell.

His lips leave mine, and then again, he says, "Breathe."

I do but only because he said so. It's no longer an automatic response for me. I'm too consumed by his kisses to even do something as simple as breathing.

He laughs. "This is going to be far too enjoyable for me, Olive."

He takes a step back and then another, leaving me feeling empty and alone even though he's only a few feet from me. He takes a seat in a chair in the corner. I walk forward, assuming he wants me in his lap, kissing him further.

"Stop."

I do—not because I want to, but because I can't help but give in to him when he says words in his sexy voice. I can't think straight enough to come up with a coherent argument for me to keep moving.

"Undress for me."

That seems to break the spell. Because, as much as I want to have sex with him, the thought of having to undress in front of him while he inspects every inch of my body terrifies me. He's built like a Greek god. I can see that without him ever removing an ounce of clothing. While I'm skinny, I'm an assistant who spends far more time at work than I do in a gym. I like cooking and baking and eating far too much to slowly undress in front of him.

"Why don't you remove my clothes? It will be far more enjoyable for you to rip them off my body," I say. I'm hoping that, if he has his hands on me, he won't be able to get a good look at my body and imperfections.

Sean frowns. "You gave up control, remember? Now, strip slowly for me, or you won't get what you want. And, trust me, you want what I'm going to give you, Olive. Because I guarantee you, no man has made you come like I'm going to. But, first, you have to pay the price."

I don't know how he does it, but his voice makes me change my mind. It makes me want what he promises. So, I move my hands to the buttons on my shirt, and I pop open the first one and then another and another until the shirt hangs open on my body. When I'm finished, I look up at Sean, who is waiting patiently for me to take off my shirt.

"Take off your shirt."

I meet his gaze as I slowly slip off my shirt. I let the shirt fall to the floor and show the first level of imperfections that grace my body—the large birthmark on half of my stomach and the large scar on the other half where my gallbladder was removed. He sees the weight that I'm still carrying from Christmas when I ate a few too many chocolates and drank a little too much wine to deal with my family.

It's just the first layer. Soon, when I remove my bra, he will see that I wear a push-up bra to make my boobs look bigger. When I remove the skirt, he'll see the cellulite and stretch marks that cover my ass, something that I know a man like him has never seen on the models I'm sure he usually dates.

When I look at his eyes going over what little of my body is exposed, I don't see him finding my imperfections. His eyes tell me how much he doesn't care about them and how much he still wants to fuck me. I wait for some smirk or comment. For him to tell me that he's changed his mind.

Instead, he says, "I want more."

I grab my skirt and slowly shimmy it down my body until it falls around my ankles while I continue to stare into his eyes.

"Step closer. I want to get a closer look at you."

I suck in a breath and then take a step forward. I quickly feel myself losing my balance because my skirt is still around my ankles. I fall flat on my face on the floor. I wait for the laughter or teasing, but instead, I feel his arms around me as he lifts me up and then softly places me on the bed.

I open my eyes and see Sean looking at me with such lust and need that I forget that I just looked like an idiot in front of him. I forget that I'm half-naked and exposed in front of him.

"Fuck waiting and punishing you. I need you now."

A second later, he has my bra off and one of my nipples in his mouth. I moan loudly as his tongue swirls around my nipple.

He sucks hard. "You like that, baby?"

"Yes," I say, half-breathing, half-moaning.

His lips move to my other breast, giving it the same attention he just gave the other. "Fuck, your tits are perfect, Olive."

"Don't stop!" I scream.

He continues to torture my breasts, bringing me ever-so close to coming from just what he is doing to my boobs.

He grins against my breast and then says, "But, if I don't stop, then how am I going to do this?" He grabs my panties and sharply pulls them down. He grabs my legs and opens them wide before burying his face in my pussy.

I've never had a man go down on me before. Sure, I've had boyfriends who have tried to get me excited with their hands, but it was nothing like what Sean is doing now. His face is buried between my legs, his tongue expertly moving in and out of my folds, inside my pussy, and then up over my clit. It's a feeling I've never felt before, and I wasn't expecting it.

I'm seconds away from coming as his tongue licks over my clit, and suddenly, his fingers bury deep inside my pussy. I scream, and he knows I'm close to coming. Just as I'm about to come, he stops. He sits up and pulls his shirt off over his body.

Yummy.

His body is beautiful. It's all abs and muscles and tan, not like my fair skin that never gets to see the light of day here in Chicago.

He walks over to the nightstand and pulls out a condom before slipping out of his jeans and underwear. As he walks back toward the bed, I turn my head away, too embarrassed to even look at him.

He laughs. "You can look, Olive."

I do even though I know my cheeks are now bright red with embarrassment. I eat him up with my eyes.

But the way he carries his body and walks toward me before climbing up on top of the bed makes me realize how much I want to be like him. It's a crazy thought that I want to be like a man I hate. But I can learn a lot from Sean. I'd love to be able to walk into a room and carry my head high, no matter what stupid things I end up doing.

"Like what you see?" he asks with a smirk.

"Yes. You like what you see?" I say bravely, shocked at myself for being so bold.

His eyes travel down my body and then back up to my eyes. "I already have your body forever etched into my memory. I love it so much."

I bite my lip, and then he shocks me by tossing me the condom and rolling over onto his back.

"Fuck me, Olive."

I can't tell if he is giving me the control or if he's keeping the control by demanding that I fuck him instead of him fucking me. Now, I'm suddenly nervous again. He clearly has much more experience than I do.

I swallow hard as I rip the condom wrapper open and take the condom out. And then I look at Sean's eyes as he dares me to prove to him that I'm not some naive, scared woman. It's just another test. It's just, this time, the test is sex.

I grab his dick harder than I should but enough to show him that I'm taking back control. And then I roll the condom down on top of it before I throw my leg over him, straddling him as my hands claw at his chest. I lower my lips to his and kiss him hard, like he did to me, before I fuck him.

I wince a little as his dick slides inside me. I'm not used to someone his size—or used to sex much anyway. I haven't had sex in over a month. Owen simply didn't have the time. Now, I know why. Owen was seeing another woman on the side. He was fucking. Just her and not me.

"Use it," Sean says with a grin.

He knows what I'm thinking, that I'm thinking about Owen. He knew I would the second I started having sex with another man who wasn't Owen. So, I do. I thrust up and down on top of Sean's dick, using my hatred for Owen, taking it out on sex with Sean. And, as good as it feels, I need Sean to help me get there again. I can't move like he does.

"What do you want, Olive? Tell me," Sean says.

"I want your tongue on my nipples again."

He sits up, and his lips cover my nipple. His tongue teases me again as it dances between my breasts while his eyes find mine. He makes me moan louder, bringing me closer but not quite there. Sean raises an eyebrow at me, challenging me to keep telling him what I want, to take control. I'm thankful to have some control again, but I know that, as I long as I keep fucking him like this, I'll never get what I want.

"Fuck me, and make me come," I say.

He grins as he grabs my hips and starts moving me up and down and in a circular motion, much faster and harder than I could on my own. His mouth stays on my tit, and I groan loud, like I've never groaned before. So loud that I'm sure the whole building heard me. He doesn't tell me to come or to quiet my screams. He just gives me one more dirty look and thrusts harder, making me scream and orgasm all over his hard dick.

It takes me a second to calm my breathing, but when I do, he says, "That was for you. This one is for me...and maybe you."

Before I have time to think, he pulls out of me and flips me over face-first onto the bed. His dick enters hard from behind me. I struggle for air as he fucks me hard against the bed. He smacks my ass hard twice. Hard enough that it brings tears to my eyes, but not so hard that I want him to stop. And then he comes hard and fast while screaming out my name before collapsing onto my back. We stay like that, stuck together, both recovering from one of the best fucks of my life.

Sean slowly gets up and says, "Want to take a shower with me? I'm sure we can find something fun to do in the shower." He winks at me.

I roll onto my back, smiling, trying to give myself a few more seconds to recuperate before I say yes to my first time getting fucked in a shower.

But then Sean's eyes grow wide as he stares at me, and I'm afraid, now that the sex goggles are gone, he sees something in me that he doesn't like.

"What?"

Sean frowns and seriously looks at me. "Olive, please tell me you weren't a virgin."

I bite my lip to try to keep from laughing because he will be far too fun to play with in this moment. I look down at the two spots of blood staining his white sheets. "It was my first time..." I say.

"Oh my God, Olive! I can't believe you tricked me like that. I would never have fucked you if I knew you were a virgin. I don't do virgins. Far too clingy, and I'm not good with all the emotions and crap..." Sean keeps rambling, but I don't hear him because I'm dying laughing at him freaking out.

"It's not funny, Olive. You need to tell a man before you let him fuck you for the first time."

I start laughing so hard that I snort. "You didn't let me finish," I say between laughs.

Sean narrows his eyes. "Of course I let you finish. You came twice if I recall. It's not my fault you don't know what an orgasm is yet."

I laugh even harder. I finally get up from the bed and shake off the laughs as I put my hand on his hard chest. "It was the first time that a man made me orgasm while having sex. Not my first time having sex. I must just be starting my period or something."

I walk past him and into the bathroom, enjoying having the upper hand for once. My jaw falls open again though when I see that the size of his bathroom is larger than my entire apartment. And the shower is big enough to comfortably hold half a dozen people at least.

I feel Sean behind me.

"You know, it's not nice to test people."

I grin as I turn and face him. "I'm just learning from the best," I say with a wink.

"I'm going to have to punish you for that."

I grin even wider. "Good. Because I think I like your punishments."

9

SEAN

I'm running away. I don't ever run away from anything, but I'm running away from Olive.

I didn't expect one night with her to affect me so much, but it did. She is so different from any woman I've ever dated before.

I enjoyed fucking her more than I'd thought I would. I know that she is inexperienced, and inexperienced women aren't usually my type, but, man, did I love breaking her, showing her what sex could be like with a real man.

But she can't get attached. I don't date women, and I sure as hell don't fuck the same woman more than once. Because that leads them to thinking that I'm willing to date them, and I'm not. The only woman I've ever considered dating again is Jamie. She's the only person I've ever really cared about. I'm not going to let another woman cause me any pain if they don't even compare to Jamie. I'm not going to put myself in that kind of pain ever again.

I've never met a woman who can compare to Jamie, but Olive and Jamie are so different that it would be hard to compare the two anyway. Jamie is confident, determined. She knows exactly what she wants and how to get it. Olive is a sweet, clumsy mass with very little confidence. But I'm also discovering how beautiful she really is, how strong, how sassy she is when she wants to be. And there's just something about Olive that I can't quite understand. She has this quality, and I don't know if I love her or hate her. She just gets under my skin in a way that no woman, even Jamie, ever has before.

I look out the window as the private jet takes off from Chicago. I never pay for private jets. They are a waste of my money since I usually just fall asleep on the plane the second that it takes off anyway. I'd rather spend my money on other things—cars, condos, expensive wine and food. But, today, I just need a plane with no one else on it. One that will take me wherever I want, mainly away from Chicago and Olive.

I need to put some space between me and her now because nothing else is going to happen between us. We had our one night of fun, and now, it's back to business. And I need Olive to know that because, if she fucks up one time, she's gone. I'm not giving her any special treatment just because I like fucking her.

The copilot comes back toward me after we've taken off. "Mr. Burrows, it's a ten-hour flight to San Paolo. Are you sure you're only going to need three hours after we arrive before wanting to return, sir?"

"Yes."

"Okay, sir. We will have the plane ready to turn around three hours after we land," the copilot says, closely studying me before heading back to the cockpit.

He knows better than to question why we're flying all this way to a place that I don't even have any business ties to. He doesn't understand, that's the point. This weekend isn't about business or women. This weekend is about getting away and making me forget about Olive even if that means wasting money and spending most of my time in the air, drinking and sleeping.

I lean my chair back and close my eyes, trying to sleep—

something that I didn't get any of last night because I spent all my time fucking Olive or watching her as she slept, trying my best to understand her. But, the more I tried to understand her, the more intrigued I became with her.

I try to sleep and think of something else, anything other than Olive, but my brain automatically goes to her. It's eight o'clock. She's probably just waking up and finding the note I left her. She's probably mad, cursing my name because I left her all alone after I fucked her. I hate that I'm hurting her, but it's better to hurt her now than a year from now, like Owen did.

And, for once, I need to look out for myself. That's what I've learned after all these years. No one else is going to look out for me, so I have to. And I always put me first. And, right now, what I need is to just be gone.

10

OLIVE

Sean's gone.

I know it without opening my eyes. He thought he was being sneaky this morning when he snuck out of bed, threw on clothes, and then typed a message onto my phone. He thought I was sound asleep. That he had fucked me so hard last night that I wouldn't even be able to function until hours later.

But he doesn't know me at all.

I grin. Well, he knows me a little bit. He knows the sound I make when he enters me. He knows the look on my face when I come. He knows every imperfection on my body. He knows exactly how to fuck me. He just doesn't know me.

He doesn't know that I'm used to waking up early. That I hardly ever get any sleep.

But, when he left early this morning, I acted like I was asleep. I didn't let him know that I was awake. I'm not going to become a clingy girl who needs him to basically propose to me the morning after. I got what I needed out of him. Sex. And, now, it's time to forget about Owen.

Honestly, right now, I appreciate that there will be some

distance between us. The distance will help with the awkwardness when I see him at work on Monday.

I stretch and yawn as I roll over to grab my phone and read the message he left for me.

"Ow," I moan as I move. *Damn, I'm sore.*

I click on the message and read it.

I got a call. I need to handle some emergencies that came up at work. Help yourself to any food you can find in the condo. Your training will continue Monday.

—Sean

I sigh. He lied to me. He didn't get a call this morning. He just jumped out of bed like it was on fire, and he couldn't get out of here fast enough.

I read through the message several more times, searching for any kind of clue as to what Sean does for a living or how he feels about me. But I find nothing, no matter how many times I read it.

He gives no clue to what he does for a living, and it's pretty obvious how he feels about me. He fucked me, and now, he's done with me. I'm going to be lucky if I even still have a job on Monday. Because I have a feeling that, if I fuck up at work, then I'm done. He doesn't need the hassle. Plus, if I'm gone, then he can hire a new assistant he can fuck.

He said I could help myself to his food, but I have a better idea.

I get out of bed, shivering immediately from the cold air. I wrap my arms around my body and begin searching the floor for my clothes, but I can't find them. I sigh. *Shit.* I'm going to have to wear some of his clothes out of here.

I walk toward the bathroom and then stop when I see a white robe hanging in the doorway that wasn't there before. I hesitantly pull the robe off the hanger like it's going to bite me or something and then put it on.

"Oh my God!" I moan as I wrap the soft robe around my body. It's the softest, most comfortable thing I have ever worn. I walk into the bathroom and find my clothes nicely folded up on the counter.

Did Sean do that?

He must have because no one else came into the room to collect them, just like he must have put out the robe for me, knowing I would be cold the second I stepped out of the bedroom. I blink, thinking I've imagined this. That the same guy who flipped me over and fucked me against the bed just for him last night would do something so considerate as folding my clothes and putting out a robe blows my mind.

I don't understand Sean any more than he understands me.

I grin. But I know how Sean looks naked, I know how his tongue can do things to me I never thought were possible, and I know how hard his dick is when it drives inside me. And that is all I care to know about Sean. Everything else doesn't matter. I already know that he is a jerk in every way that matters. He just happens to be better than any man I've ever fucked combined in bed.

I decide to just wear the robe while I go in search of breakfast, but as I walk down the hallway to the main open room, I stop at a door that I don't remember seeing when Sean led me to his bedroom last night. Curious, I open the door, but I'm let down when I see just a large desk sitting in the center of the room, looking out the large floor-to-ceiling windows, instead of a sex dungeon or some other crazy thing that I imagine Sean having.

I start walking toward the kitchen, my stomach leading the way, when my curiosity gets the better of me. I walk back to his office and sit down at his desk. I glance up in the corners of the room, looking for a camera or some sort of security system that is watching me, but I find none.

It doesn't mean they aren't there, I think.

I sit for a minute, trying to decide if my curiosity is worth the punishment that Sean is going to give me if he finds out that I searched through his office.

It's worth it.

I start opening drawers, searching through papers and files, looking for anything that will let me know what Sean does for a living when he's not running Jamie's company. Because, as much as I wish that I didn't care at all about figuring out Sean, I do care. At least, I care enough to find out what dark, dirty thing he does to make the millions that he has

———

I don't know what Sean does for a living, and I'm afraid I might never know. My curiosity is going to kill me if I don't find out though. I spent three hours searching through his condo for any clue, but I found none. Not one damn thing that pointed me in any sort of direction.

My phone doesn't get reception while riding the L train, so I couldn't even spend my ride home looking him up. Instead, my mind came up with all sorts of crazy things. *He's in the mob. He sells drugs. He's a porn star.*

Everything that I came up with just made me more and more concerned that, whatever Sean does, it isn't good. I need to text Jamie. She knows what Sean does. Surely, she wouldn't let him run the company if he was into illegal stuff. Would she?

I climb up the seven flights of stairs to my apartment since the elevator is still broken—and most likely, always will be. I unlock the door and step inside, still thinking about Sean.

"Where have you been? I've been going crazy here!" Keri says as I walk into my one-room loft.

After seeing Sean's place, I feel even more like I live in a closet. My kitchen has a fridge that barely fits a bottle of wine, a microwave that also functions as an oven, one burner plate, and three cabinets for storage. The rest of the room consists of a small TV balanced on top of a trunk filled with my clothes, and sitting across from it is my daybed that also functions as my couch. The door to the bathroom is next to my bed where I have a toilet and a shower that I can barely turn around in. The only nice part about my apartment is the balcony that I can barely fit a chair on, but if I sit out there and squint really hard while tilting my head to one side, then I can see Lake Michigan from between the buildings.

"What are you doing here?" I ask.

Keri shakes her head. "No. You answer me first. I was this close to calling the police to report you missing!" she says, moving her index finger and thumb close together.

"I was with Sean," I say, as I put my purse down.

"Who?" Keri asks.

I blush just a little. "My boss."

Now, Keri's eyes grow big. "Why didn't you answer any of my messages then? It's not like he took you to Antarctica or someplace that doesn't have any reception!" Keri yells at me.

I pull my phone out of my purse and blush, more embarrassed that I didn't even notice that I had any messages from anyone other than Sean.

"Oh my God!" Keri says slowly as she realizes what happened. "You let him fuck you, didn't you?" She throws up her hands. "I can't believe you. I give up on you, Olive. I've really tried to get you to see your own self-worth and to stop dating these horrible guys who do nothing but hurt you, but you have to help yourself, too!"

"Sean didn't hurt me. Owen did, but Sean didn't! I knew what I was getting into with Sean."

"How could he not? He fucked you and then left you, didn't he? They all do."

I frown. "But, unlike Owen, he was up-front and told me he was going to leave me. I knew what I was getting into with Sean. I don't even like him! I just needed some mind-blowing sex! I just needed something to make me forget about what Owen did."

Keri shakes her head. "It might not hurt now. But I know you, Olive. What happens when you want this guy to take you out to dinner or hold your hand during a romantic movie, and he says no? Then, how are you going to feel?"

My frown deepens. She really is never going to understand how I feel. That, for once in my life, I made the right decision for myself and not the wrong one.

I dig my phone out of my purse and search *Sean Burrows* on my phone and wait for his image to show up, and then I push the phone in her face. "Do you really think I thought a guy like this was going to be into anything more than a one-time fuck? And do you really think I would pass up an opportunity to fuck a guy like Sean?"

"Holy shit!" Keri says, grabbing the phone from me. "You really fucked him?" she asks, not able to tear her eyes away from the image that really doesn't even do him justice.

I grin. "Yes."

"Oh my God! Tell me everything! Was he as amazing in bed as I imagine him to be?"

"Better."

"No way!" Keri says, typing something on my phone.

"What are you doing?" I ask.

"Sending the picture to my phone," Keri says with a smile.

I roll my eyes and grab my phone back before walking over

and taking a seat on my daybed. I grab one of the pillows and squeeze it in my lap while Keri sits down next to me.

"As much as I want to hear more about Sean, I have to ask you about Owen. What happened? He called me last night, frantic that you had gone crazy and said you broke up with him. That's why I came over last night."

That's when I notice that my bed isn't made, and it's clear that Keri spent the night sleeping in my bed.

"He kissed another girl in a bar on our anniversary. So, I broke up with him. He's a douche bag, just like you always said he was."

Keri looks down, not meeting my eyes.

"What are you not telling me?" I ask.

Keri slowly looks up at me. "It's just...are you sure he was cheating on you?"

I jump up in disbelief at what Keri is suggesting. "You can't be serious! You've hated Owen since the day I first started dating him! Of course he was cheating on me! I saw it with my own eyes! He was making out with another girl!"

Keri gets up. "I know, I know. But you didn't hear him on the phone last night, Olive. He was...heartbroken."

"So what? I hope he was heartbroken. How do you think I felt when I found him with his lips locked on another girl?"

Keri sighs. "I know, Olive. It must have felt horrible. But...but what if you were wrong?"

"How could I have been wrong? I saw him kissing another girl!"

She nods. "But was it a quick kiss or a full make-out session?"

"Why does it matter? He was kissing another girl!"

"What if the girl he was with was his sister?"

I laugh. "That's sick if it was his sister. They were making out!"

She shakes her head. "Were they? You just said a second ago that you couldn't remember if they were making out or if it was just one quick kiss."

My head is pounding as I think about Owen as I pace around the room. "They were definitely making out."

Keri grabs my arms, forcing me to stop pacing around the room and look at her. "I seriously doubt that. Because I know for a fact that it was his sister who was with him last night. And, since I didn't get any weird vibes from them when they came over here together, I seriously doubt they were making out. It was more than likely just some friendly quick kiss between siblings."

I shake my head. "I know what I saw. He was cheating on me with that bitch."

Keri sighs. "No, he wasn't."

I shake her hands off me. "And how would you know?"

"Because he came over here, and I talked to him. I talked to his sister. She's really a nice person. And, while Owen hasn't always treated you the best, after talking to him last night, I do really think that he loves you and will try to do better in taking care of you."

I shake my head. "That's not possible. He doesn't love me. He's treated me like dirt all these months we have been together," I say as strongly as I can, but my voice breaks.

"Olive...he was going to propose last night. That's why his sister is in town. She brought him their grandmother's ring. He was going to propose to you last night. And how he was going to do it was good, Olive. He went all out with fireworks, a carriage ride, the whole bit."

"But..." I can't speak as my legs give out beneath me.

Keri catches me, and we both slink down to the floor.

I stare at Keri as one tear escapes from my eye. "Are you sure? You're sure he didn't cheat on me?"

Keri nods.

"You're sure he was going to propose?"

She nods again.

"You really think he loves me?"

She exhales. "Yes."

"Fuck."

Keri laughs. "Oh, honey! This is a good thing. Owen is finally stepping up and showing that he really cares about you. You could finally be getting everything you want. You're going to get married to a man who loves you. A man who can support you and take care of you. You don't have to be alone anymore. You don't have to live in this shithole anymore."

I know her words are meant to comfort me, but they are doing the exact opposite. Twenty-four hours ago, I wanted nothing more than for Owen to propose. I would have said yes. I would have done anything for him. But that was before Sean. Before I realized that I like rough, dirty sex that leaves me wanting more. I don't like boring sex with Owen, who doesn't even know how everything works. I want a man who knows my body just as well as he knows my soul.

"It doesn't matter now. I slept with Sean. Owen won't want to marry me now."

Keri frowns. "I wouldn't say that. He doesn't even have to know if you don't want him to."

I look at Keri, feeling a little empty. "I'm not going to lie to him. But, honestly, I'm not sure that I want Owen anymore."

Keri's eyes widen again as she gently strokes my back. "What? Are you sure? I don't think this Sean guy is going to be dating material. He might be hot, but I doubt he will want anything serious."

I shake my head. "It's not because of Sean. I'm just not afraid to be alone anymore. I don't need a man to be happy."

Keri doesn't move or say anything. She just stares at me.

I start clicking my tongue as I call for my cat, "Here, Milo." I search for my kitty under the bed where he usually likes to hang out. But I don't find him there. "Where's Milo?" I ask Keri.

She frowns and bites her lip.

"What happened to him?" I ask, jumping up.

"Relax. Owen took him. He said he bought the cat. That he was his, and he needed the comfort in a time like this."

"And you just let him take him?" I scream at Keri as I run toward my door to grab my purse and some sort of jacket. I froze on the L train on the way over here, and I'm not going to do it again. I open the door just as a delivery person knocks.

"Are you Olive?" the man asks.

I nod. "Yes."

He hands me a package, and I step back inside for a second to open it. I pull out the coat. It's gorgeous. It's Gucci. It's expensive. I slip it on as a note falls to the floor. I pick it up and read it.

A coat fit for a boss. Prove to me that you are one.

—Sean

I smile at the note. He got me an expensive coat. A beautiful coat that costs three times what my rent is.

"How did you afford that coat?" Keri asks.

I frown as I look at her. "Sean."

Keri blinks several times but doesn't say anything.

I grab my phone and begin typing a message to Jamie. Now, more than anything, I need to know what Sean does. I have to know how I hate a man that I also kind of love. He's taken care of me more in the last few hours, not even being near me, than Owen did the whole year we were dating.

I press Send and then walk out the door with Keri running behind me.

"Where are you going?" she asks.

"To get my cat back and to make sure that Owen knows we are still broken up."

11

———

SEAN

FUCK, I'm hungover.

And tired.

No, exhausted.

I could sleep for another week straight and still not get enough sleep. I thought I'd feel better after spending the last forty-eight hours doing nothing but sleeping and drinking. But I was wrong. All it did was make me feel worse. I feel no more rested than I was when I left, and I haven't gotten the images of Olive out of my head any more than I could before I left.

So, that's why I'm taking some drastic measures. I can't get Olive out of my head, and I'm not sure if abandoning her in my apartment and not calling her is going to be enough to really make her hate me. I'm going to tell Olive the truth about what I do for a living. That's the only solution I've come up with. If I tell her what I do for a living, then she'll hate me. And, if she hates me, she won't want to fuck me again. Problem solved. I might even get lucky, and she might quit.

Then, I can focus on what I really came here to do. Run a successful real estate company and to see if I still have a shot with Jamie. And, if I don't have a chance with her, then I need to learn to get over her.

I step foot inside the office and expect it to be bustling with people, as it usually is on a weekday. I've learned from my week here and from speaking with Jamie on the phone that Monday through Friday are the busiest office days while the weekends are the busiest days for the realtors to be doing open houses and showing houses to clients. And my role as the boss is to get people straightened out during the week so that they can do their best at selling the most houses over the weekend.

But I don't expect what I see when I enter the office. I was expecting the office to be a bit chaotic on Monday morning after a busy weekend and since I wasn't here over the weekend to ensure that everything was running smoothly. But what I see when I walk into the office is complete chaos. People are running around everywhere with no clue as to what they're doing. Papers are flying and strewed all over desks in complete and utter disorganization. But that's not what worries me. Disorganization, I can easily fix. What scares me is the look on everyone's faces as they run around the office. Something's not right.

"What's going on?" I ask Jennifer, one of the realtors, as she walks by.

She stops and looks up at me with fear in her eyes. "It's Monday?" she half-asks and half-says, but I know it's not the truth.

I sigh and continue walking to my office. I need answers, and I know the only woman who is going to give me any sort of honest answer as to what the hell is going on is Olive. And, as much as I'd rather hide in my office all day and wait to talk to her until later, it doesn't seem that I'm going to get to wait.

I walk straight to her desk, but she's not there. I glance at my watch. It's a quarter till nine. Olive is always here by this time. Usually, she's already been here at least an hour or more. I glance around the office to see if I can find her. But I don't see her anywhere, and I don't know where to start looking.

Floyd walks over. "Where is Olive?" he asks.

"I was wondering that myself."

Floyd's face turns to panic. "Shit."

"What?" I say a little too sternly.

Floyd's eyes dart from Olive's desk to my eyes. "It's just that there's only been one other time when Olive was sick with the flu and didn't come in to work. Happened about two years ago, and it was the worst week. Nobody sold any properties that week. It's like she's a good-luck charm or something. Or she put a curse on this place, and we can only sell properties as long as she is here."

"What makes you think Olive is sick?" I ask.

"Do you see her anywhere?" Floyd says, annoyed.

He runs out to do God knows what while I stand, frozen, staring at the chaos. I'm beginning to think that the reason for the chaos might be because Olive isn't here.

I haven't had enough time this week to really see what Olive contributes to the team, but it seems she might contribute more than I ever gave her credit for. But whatever it is that she contributes, even if it's as simple as just providing stability and normalcy for the rest of the employees, I'm going to figure it out.

But, in the meantime, there's one thing I know for sure. Olive isn't sick. She's avoiding me. She's too embarrassed to come into work after she let her boss bang her.

I stop the next person who walks by even though I don't know her name. "Can you tell me Olive's address?"

The woman shrugs. "No, but I'm sure Jamie has it somewhere."

I pull out my phone as I walk into my office. I try Olive's number first, but I get no answer. She is definitely avoiding me. I frown. It's like everything I've taught her has already gone out the window. I'm fine with Olive quitting or thinking this isn't the position for her. I'm not fine with her hiding. She doesn't get to take the easy way out. I need her to fight for what she wants. So, I text Jamie and head back out to find Olive. And I hope that, in the meantime, the company doesn't come to a crashing halt.

———

I pull up in front of her apartment building, but I can't believe that this is where she lives. Jamie must have made a mistake when she sent me her address. I try calling Jamie and Olive, but neither of them answers. So, it leaves me no choice but to go inside and see for myself that this isn't her place.

The apartment building doesn't have a valet or parking garage that I can find, so I have to circle the box three times before I find any sort of street parking that's close. Although, after seeing the neighborhood that she loves, I really wish I had taken a cab and left my car back in the parking garage at the office.

I jump out of my car and run inside the building, determined to make this as quick as possible so that nothing happens to my car. I head over to the elevator and see the large sign that says it is out of order.

Really? How can an elevator be out of order in an apartment building this tall?

I dash over to the stairs and run up, quickly taking them two at a time, struggling for breath. I might be in shape. I run and lift, but I'm not used to climbing stairs like this. When I finally make it to her floor, I'm sweating and out of breath. This is ridiculous. I've done all this, and I still don't think she lives here.

I walk over to the door that is supposedly hers and knock, and I don't hear any movement inside. I knock one more time before I decide to give up. But, just as I'm about to leave, the door opens, and Olive stares at me, wide-eyed, in the doorway.

"What...how...what are you doing here?" Olive asks, crossing her arms.

I grin, thankful that I finally found the right place. "Aren't you going to invite me in?"

"No."

"Fine. Then, I have no choice but to believe that the reason you called in sick today is because of me. That you're too embarrassed to see me again after we fucked."

Olive frowns but opens the door wider, and I slip inside. I stare around the small place that she calls an apartment. But that's obviously not what it is. It's a closet or storage room. It's definitely too small to be an apartment. I look around for a place to sit, but there is none. Because every inch of space in her apartment is filled with cookies, brownies, cakes, or muffins. I glance over at what is supposed to be her kitchen and have no idea how she's made this many bakery items in such a small kitchen that I'm not even sure functions any better than one of those Easy-Bake ovens that kids use.

If this is all she can afford, she's definitely not getting paid enough. Especially now that I know that, for some reason, the company practically falls apart without her there. But I'm not going to tell her that—at least, not yet. Not until I know that she has the confidence to actually earn the respect and that they think of her as a boss and not just a good-luck charm.

"Yeah, looks like you're sick to me," I say.

Olive glares at me. "I am sick."

I look around at all the bakery items. "Then, why are you baking if you're sick? Shouldn't you be in bed? And aren't you going to have to throw out everything now that they are contaminated with your sickness?"

An alarm goes off, and Olive walks over to the tiny oven. She pulls out a small pan of brownies and places it on the only space left on the counter. Then, she throws the dish towel at me. "Baking makes me happy. It relaxes me."

"Relaxing won't help you get over whatever sickness you have."

"Migraines. I get migraines, especially when I'm stressed."

"So, you're telling me that I gave you a migraine?" I say, smiling.

She takes the tray of cookies off what I can't tell is either a couch or bed and sits down, plopping the tray on her lap. She takes one of the cookies off the tray and starts eating it. "No, I don't have a migraine because of you. I don't care that you left me alone this weekend and didn't call me. I'm not too embarrassed to go to work because I fucked my boss."

I raise an eyebrow, waiting for her to continue because I just don't believe her.

She sighs. "I'm anxious and stressed because Owen won't give me my cat, Milo, back."

I narrow my eyes at her. She's never talked about a cat before, but then she does seem like the type to own a cat. Although I have no idea how two creatures could survive in such a small place.

"Have you learned nothing from me? If it's your cat, you don't have to ask permission. Just take the cat back," I say.

"I tried, but it's not as simple as that. Owen paid for the cat. I have no legal right to Milo, and he's trying to blackmail me, so I'll take him back. Because it turns out, he didn't really cheat on me. It was just a quick kiss between him and his sister. It turns out, he was going to propose."

My eyes widen when she says *propose* because Owen definitely doesn't seem like the type, and it pisses me off that anyone would think they had a claim to a woman I just fucked.

"And you don't want to marry him anymore because of me?"

She looks up from her tray of cookies as her eyes grow darker. "No, not because of you, you idiot. I don't want to marry him because I've realized that I don't really love him. I'm not ready to marry anyone yet. I want to be by myself for a while and figure out what I want without a guy. I just want my cat back."

I stare at her a second longer, trying to tell if she is telling the truth or not. "Then, let's go get him."

12

OLIVE

MY HEART IS POUNDING RIGHT ALONG with my head as Sean drives us toward Owen's apartment. Sean is talking, trying to pep me up to talk to Owen, but he doesn't understand that it isn't going to work. I've already tried talking tough to Owen. I have no legal right to the cat. And I doubt that Owen will even open the door. It's before noon. He's probably still asleep. And I was stupid enough to date a guy for a year without asking for a key to his place.

Maybe Sean will know how to break into his place, or maybe he knows the owner of the apartment complex, and he'll let us into Owen's place. I grab my head that is pounding worse than it ever has before. I shouldn't get my hopes up. I'm not getting back my cat or anything else I left at his place.

"Olive, are you listening to me?" Sean asks.

"Huh?" I say, looking at him, as he pulls the car in front of Owen's apartment building.

Sean searches my eyes for a second as the valet opens my door. "You got this, Olive. Just treat him like you would me."

I nod and get out of the car, but my legs feel unsteady the second I get out. I start walking toward the door, but between my head pounding and my legs being weak and wobbly, I know there is no way I'm going to make it without falling and embarrassing myself even more in front of Sean.

I feel myself going down when Sean catches me.

"Thank you," I say weakly.

"You should go training with me sometime. Build up some strength in your legs."

"It's not—"

Sean grabs my chin and kisses me, stopping me from thinking. I don't know how he does it, but when he kisses me, it's like he transfers some of his confidence into me. The kiss isn't meant to be loving or sexual. It's a confidence boost.

When Sean pulls away, he stares at me with a serious expression. I was expecting his sexy grin or a smirk to be smeared on his face because he knows full well that his kiss affected me. But it's not there.

I narrow my eyes as I study him and try to understand what he is feeling, but I can't. I don't know him well enough, and it's clear that he doesn't let anyone in.

So, I turn my attention away from Sean and start walking into the apartment building with his hand on the small of my back, ensuring that I'm not going to fall again. But I don't want his hand on me. I don't want his help. I want to do this on my own. So, I walk faster until Sean is no longer keeping up with me. I automatically go to the stairs instead of the elevator.

"You know this place has an actual functioning elevator, like a normal apartment should?" Sean says.

I pause at the entrance to the stairwell and turn to look at Sean. He's standing with his hands in the pockets of his gray suit pants. He looks so perfect, beautiful. He looks like a successful adult who knows what he wants in his life. Meanwhile, I'm wearing pajama pants, a sweatshirt, and the coat Sean got me. I'm a mess while he is perfectly put together.

"You have a problem with my apartment? Then, pay me more. It's the best I can afford."

One of Sean's eyebrows rises.

"I'm taking the stairs. I like the stairs. I don't like elevators," I say.

Then, I realize that I might have made a mistake because Sean's face lights up at that. He thinks he knows some deep, dark secret about me, but he doesn't. I don't like elevators. I like the burn and the time to think that climbing the stairs offers better than the silence and awkwardness that an elevator provides. That's it.

I start running up the stairs, but I don't hear Sean behind me. I finally make it to Owen's floor, and I'm completely out of breath, but it feels good. I walk out of the stairwell and down the hallway toward Owen's apartment when I see Sean leaning against the wall with a smirk on his face. I stop, completely out of breath, in front of him.

Sean leans down to my ear and says, "I like elevators better. Why waste energy on anything you don't need to? I'd rather reserve my energy for other more enjoyable things."

A shiver runs up and down my spine. I walk past Sean, ignoring his smirk and comment. I walk up to Owen's apartment door and knock loudly. I ignore what Sean is doing to my heart. I can't do this if I'm thinking about Sean.

I don't give Owen much time to come to the door before I start knocking loudly again, and this time, when I start, I can't stop. I knock on the door the same way that others might punch a pillow. It's a way to get my frustration and anger out. But, instead of making me feel weaker, the pounding on the door makes me feel stronger than ever.

I feel myself punching air as the door swings open, and Owen stands in the doorway, looking at me.

"I want my cat and stuff back," I say before Owen has a chance to say anything.

I look him up and down while I wait for him to speak to me. I no longer feel embarrassed by how I look because Owen looks worse. It's clear he just woke up, and while I have the excuse of being sick with a migraine, Owen just looks hungover and pathetic.

Owen rubs his head, like my voice was too loud for him. "What are you doing here, Olive? We already had this conversation."

"We are going to have it again and again until I get what I need, Owen."

"What you need? What about what I need, Olive? You can't just break up with a man over a misunderstanding, Olive. That's not fair!"

I laugh. "Fair? You want to talk fair? How about how, in our entire year together, you never once treated me well? We did everything your way, never mine. How fair is that? I'm not sorry that I broke up with you, Owen. I don't have to have a fair reason or any reason to break up with you. I broke up with you. Find someone else to fuck or not. I don't care. But, most importantly, give me back my cat!"

My face is red, and I'm completely out of breath. But my body is steady. I don't feel dizzy anymore. I don't feel like I'm about to faint or fall over. I feel strong.

I search Owen's eyes, but I know that he is so much of a dick that he isn't ever going to give in to me. And I know, if I involve the police, I'm going to lose. I only see one option left at getting my cat back. So, I take it.

I run as hard as I can, trying to fit between the tiny gap that Owen has left between his body and the opening to his apartment. I run and think that I've made it inside when I feel his hands come around me, pushing me back. His hands go around my neck as he pushes me back out of his apartment, and his eyes are dark with rage. I've never seen Owen so pissed off before. Not even when he was drunk and thrown out of a bar.

"You don't get to do this to me, bitch. I propose, and you marry me. I didn't throw the last year away on you to have you say no. Do you understand me?" Owen asks, his hands still firmly around my neck.

He isn't really trying to choke me, more just to contain me.

I kick him hard in the balls, and his hands immediately let go of my neck. I feel Sean walk up behind me. I look up at Sean and see an even darker rage in his eyes as he peers down at Owen.

"You're lucky that Olive got to you before I could. If you ever touch her again, I will tear your body into pieces before burying each body part on a different continent to make sure you are never found or thought of ever again," Sean says, his voice full of fury.

I look up at him, but his eyes don't soften.

"Let's get your stuff, Olive, and then get out of here," Sean says, guiding me away from where Owen is crumpled on the floor.

I step back inside Owen's apartment, and my heart is pounding so fast that I can't even think.

"Olive, where is your stuff?" Sean asks.

"Bedroom. The cat is probably also under the bed."

Sean grabs my hand and leads me that way as Owen stumbles back into the apartment. Sean pulls me into the bedroom and then locks the door behind us. He stops and strokes my face as I look up at him.

"Are you okay?" I ask, looking at the anger still in his eyes, afraid he is going to go kill Owen if we don't get out of here soon.

He laughs gently. "I should be asking you that."

I smile weakly. "I'm fine because of you."

He shakes his head. "No. You're more than fine because of you."

His lips gently find mine again, like he's afraid to roughly touch me because he might break me.

"You can kiss me harder than that. I won't break," I say.

He takes a deep breath. "I know. You're stronger than I ever thought possible. And you've learned something."

I cock my head to one side. "What?"

"You said you weren't sorry."

I grin widely. "Well, I'm not, and he needed to know that. We should get my stuff and get out of here."

I turn and head toward the closet to grab the couple of items that I have stored there when Sean grabs my hand and pulls me back to him.

"No, I think we have more important things to do first."

His lips crash down on mine, and his tongue pushes into my mouth. My whole body comes alive again when he kisses me. It's a strange feeling that I thought I would never feel again. I thought we were done after the last time. Evidently, Sean has changed his mind. And I'm more than happy to go along with his new plan until he pushes me back onto Owen's bed.

"No! We can't," I whisper as my eyes grow large.

Sean removes his suit jacket and then slowly undoes the buttons on his shirt. "I want you, Olive. Watching you put Owen in his place was a major turn-on."

Sean removes his shirt, and all I can think about is how I want to feel his hard body on mine again.

"What better way to get back at Owen than by fucking in his bed?" Sean asks, his eyes full of hunger and need.

It doesn't take any convincing for me to decide that I want him to fuck me on Owen's bed.

"Is that what you want, Olive? For me to fuck you?"

I nod as Sean undoes the buttons on my coat and pushes it off.

"You want me to touch you like he never did?"

I nod as Sean undoes the button and zipper on his pants.

"You want me to make you scream like Owen never could?"

"Yes," I breathe.

Sean takes his cock out of his pants and holds it in his hand. He pulls a condom out of his back pocket and slips it on while he stares at me the whole time.

Sean grabs my pajama pants and pulls them down hard, and I squeal just a little bit. And then I bite my lip when I realize I was far too loud for what we are about to do.

"Don't bite your lip. I want to hear every dirty moan."

He grabs my legs and spreads them wide. He buries his face between them. His tongue makes me forget about how angry I was just a second ago. I try to keep my senses about me to remain quiet because, even now, I don't want to get hurt. I don't want to become a monster, and that's what I'll feel like if I scream and make what we're doing in Owen's bed apparent.

But that's not an option.

Sean's tongue is moving faster than I ever remember him moving it before. He slides a finger into my pussy and then another and another, stretching me wide, while his other hand slips under my top until it finds my nipple, flicking across it.

The sensation is too much for me to contain, so I scream, "Fuck, more!"

But Sean stops as soon as I say *more*. "You don't get to come without me inside you. He needs to know exactly what I can do to you."

Sean pushes his cock inside me, and I grab his face, meeting his lips to try to keep my moaning at bay. But Sean only kisses me once on the lips, and then his lips move to my neck. His lips kiss up and down my neck and then nibble on my ear as he continues to affect me.

"I want to hear you scream my name."

He thrusts harder, fucking me harder and harder into the bed. I've never been fucked this hard or this fast before in my life, but it makes me want to have sex like this again and again. Harder, faster, like animals.

"Scream my name, Olive," Sean says again.

He fucks me harder and faster, to a level that I didn't know existed, until I can barely breathe or think. Until all I can do is scream.

"Sean!" I scream as I come, clawing my nails into his back.

He continues to fuck me hard and fast, each thrust harder, until he thrusts one last time, coming inside me with a force I've never felt before.

Just as I'm about to take a breath, I hear a loud pop, and then the bed collapses to the floor. I scream again as Sean's arms protectively wrap around me as we fall to the floor.

I look up at Sean, and we both laugh at the bed that is now in a collapsed mess on the floor.

"Milo!" I say, looking around for my cat, hoping to God that he wasn't under the bed in his usual hiding place.

Sean rolls off me and begins cleaning himself up while I pull my pants up. I run, searching around the room for my cat. I open the closet door and find him trapped inside, lying in the corner of the closet. I smile as I pick him up and cuddle him in my arms. He meows and nuzzles his head up against my face, happy to see me.

I look back at Sean as he pulls his pants back up. I just had him, but I want him again. Now. I take a deep breath, hoping that feeling will pass, but it only intensifies as I look at him. My headache is gone, and I feel alive for the first time since he last fucked me. He's turned me into a sex-craving lunatic.

But it's not just the sex that I want. I want him. I want the guy who, even while he was trying to keep his distance, still took care of me. If he can do that while pretending not to care, I want to know what it's like for him to truly care about somebody.

Damn it, what has he done to me?

13

SEAN

WHAT THE FUCK have I done?

I keep can't keep having sex with Olive. I'll ruin her. Because I can never love her. Not when my heart is already taken. And she needs someone to love her.

But I can't seem to stay away from her. The first time was for fun and was harmless, but this time was a relapse, one that I can never repeat again, no matter the fact that I so desperately want to.

"Do you have everything?" I ask Olive, who is firmly clutching her cat with a large smile on her face.

"Just one second," she says as she searches through the closet and finds a couple of items of clothing. She finds a small bag in the closet and puts all the items into it. Then, she picks up her coat, putting it on as she stares at the broken bed. "I feel kind of bad about the bed," she says, looking at it and then back at me.

I pick up my jacket and put it on. Then, I dig into my wallet. I pull out several hundreds and throw them onto the bed. "There. Now, he can buy a new one," I say.

She stares at the hundred-dollar bills, and I know she wants to ask about my job again, but she doesn't. Instead, she just puts the bag with her things over her shoulder and then picks up her cat again. She deliberately walks toward the door and opens it. Owen stands in the doorway, glaring at her.

I know that she didn't hear Owen screaming and pounding on the door when I was fucking her. She was too much in her own world, oblivious to anything else other than me. And that's how I wanted it.

Owen pushes past Olive and into the bedroom. His eyes grow wide as he sees the state of his bed. "What the fuck did you do to my bed?" Owen shouts at Olive.

"We fucked. He made me come and scream like you never could." Olive cocks her head to one side with a sly smile on her face. "But then I'm sure you heard that part."

Owen takes a step toward Olive, and I can't stand the thought of him going near her again, so I step in front of him, stopping him from moving any closer to her.

"Don't you dare touch her," I say.

"I should call the police. This is breaking and entering. And, now, you can add damaged property to that list of laws you broke," Owen says.

I take a step toward him so that he can feel how much stronger I am when I stand over him. "Call the police. I dare you. It will be your word against ours. And I'll tell the police how much of a piece of shit you are to put your hands on a woman like that."

Owen steps back, but he doesn't say anything. He doesn't argue with me, but I'm still not sure he gets it.

"Leave Olive the hell alone. Don't call her. Don't try to contact her. Do you understand?"

Owen's eyes dart from Olive's and then back to mine before he nods slowly.

I walk to Olive, putting my hand on the small of her back

and guiding her to the front door of the apartment. I stop for just a second and turn to Owen who has started following us.

"There should be more than enough cash on your bed to cover the damages," I say with a smirk before Olive and I leave.

"You have to promise me something, Olive," I say as we walk down the hallway.

"What's that?" she asks, snuggling with her kitty, only half-listening to me.

I stop her and force her to look up at me so that she can see how serious and important this is. She gives me her full attention when she sees the intensity in my eyes.

"You have to promise me that you will stay far away from him. Guys like Owen turn into crazy exes who do crazy things, and I just want you to be safe. So, promise me, you'll stay away, and if you do have to talk to him again, bring me."

She laughs. "What happened to me being independent and strong and standing up for myself?" she asks.

"I already know that you can do that. You being safe is more important. I just need you to be safe," I say, stroking her cheek.

"Okay, I promise," she says, staring at me with eyes that show me how much she wants me.

"Take the elevator with me," I say.

She cocks her head to one side and looks at me with narrowed eyes. "What? Why?"

"Just trust me."

She bites her lip and then sighs, "Okay."

I smile and grab her hand as we run down the hallway, toward the elevator. I know before we even reach the elevator how much of a mistake this is. I'm going to regret it as soon as it happens, but I don't care. Right now, all I can do is think with my dick instead of my head.

I press the elevator button, and then we wait while Olive holds on to her cat, studying me like I'm going crazy.

The elevator door opens a second later, and I make my intentions very clear. I push Olive into the elevator. I take the cat out of her arms and place him on the ground along with the bag that she has been carrying over her shoulder. I kiss her like I'm desperate for her, like this is the last time I'll ever be able to kiss her again. Because it just might be. Each time I kiss her or fuck her, it should be the last time, so that's how I consider it—like it's the last time.

My hand slips inside her pajama pants and panties until I find her spot between her folds that will make her forget about the fact that we're riding down in an elevator and that anyone could step on at any moment and see my hand down her pants.

I lean back and click the button for the ground floor. Then, I whisper into her ear as my fingers rub over her clit, "You have until we get to the ground floor to come. But don't worry, baby; I'll make you come long before we get there."

I watch as she sucks in a breath. Her cheeks flush pink, and she closes her eyes, trying to keep in the sudden sensation I'm causing inside her.

But she can still get words out. "But what if someone gets on the elevator before we can get to the ground?"

I bite her earlobe, making her let go of the tiny bit of control she was holding on to. "Then, you'd better come fast."

I slip a finger into her pussy while I keep rubbing against her clit. I kiss down her neck, loving the moans. I love how I can control her, make her think anything, make her do anything that I want. I can even make her stop breathing. I've never been with a woman whom I've had such control over—at least when it comes to sex. I just wish I had the same control over the rest of her, too.

I bring her close to coming over and over, but I don't let her come until we're almost to the ground floor, just one floor above.

"Come, baby," I say.

She comes, screaming my name again, while grabbing my hair, clawing at my body, as she completely loses control.

I slip my hand out of her panties just as the door is opening, and then I put my fingers in my mouth, sucking her juices off them.

Olive's eyes grow wide. She looks from me to the elevator door opening where I'm sure there's someone standing. I firmly kiss her on the lips and then pick up the bag from the floor before scooping up her cat and placing it in her arms.

Then, I grab her hand and lead her out of the elevator, not even paying attention to the people who are staring at us with disgust on their faces. I don't care what they think. I got to make Olive come again. I got to hear her sexy voice as she screamed. I got to feel her body one last time.

I watch Olive breathing quickly while we wait for the valet to bring my car around. She is still breathing hard and fast five minutes later when we both climb into the car. Her cat immediately curls up into a circle in her lap, feeling perfectly comfortable in my car.

I start driving, already knowing exactly where we're going, but I know that Olive is going to ask me soon where we are going.

"Where are we going?" she asks just a second later when she realizes I'm not heading in the direction of her apartment.

"Vegas."

"We can't go to Vegas! We have to work...the company. I don't have any clothes or things packed. I'm wearing pajamas, for Christ's sake!"

I grin. "Are you finished?"

She frowns. "No, I'm not finished. My life isn't like yours. I just can't up and decide to leave. I have people who rely on me. I need to work for money, unlike some people."

I pull out my phone, pressing one of my assistant's numbers.

When she answers, I say, "I need you to go to Olive's apartment and gather her things to go to Vegas for a few days. And then I need you to go to my condo and do the same thing. Make sure the jet is ready to go in an hour."

I hang up the phone without waiting for her to respond because I already know that it's going to be done. That's her job to make sure that she gets done whatever I tell her to.

"There. Does that make you happy?"

"No, it doesn't make me happy. How will your assistant know what to bring me?"

"Because it's her job to know things like that. You will have everything you need and everything your cat needs to go to Vegas for a couple of days."

"Why are we going to Vegas? What's so important that we need to go there? Because I can already see, you're slipping on your rule about having sex only one time."

I frown. "Don't worry; I won't slip up again—at least, not until you know everything important there is to know about me."

She raises an eyebrow. "And what is that?"

I look at her. "I'm going to show you what I do for a living."

That will solve the problem. When she knows what I do for a living, she'll hate me again.

"And I'm going to give you your final lesson before I make my decision about if you're right for the manager job."

If she doesn't decide to leave first.

14

OLIVE

I TRY NOT to care about the fact that Sean is basically kidnapping me or that I don't get a say in my life with him any more than I did with Owen. I should learn my lesson and take back control. Let Sean know that he doesn't get to control me. Let him know that no one controls my life but me.

But there is a difference between giving up control to Sean versus Owen. The difference is, I kind of like it when Sean takes control, whereas I hated it when Owen did. When Sean takes control, I know that he has my best interests at heart while Owen couldn't have cared less. Plus, Sean helped me get rid of Owen and get my cat back. I should go along with him to thank him.

But the real reason I'm going along with his crazy plan is because he told me that I'd get to find out what he does for a living. I know curiosity can lead me down dangerous paths. I just hope that my curiosity doesn't get me into too much trouble this time.

Sean pulls up in front of a building near an airport. I didn't really believe him when he told his assistant to get the jet ready. I thought maybe he just meant to get us a flight to Vegas. I didn't believe that Sean actually owned a jet. I'm still not convinced yet that he does. Maybe we're just catching a ride on someone else's small plane.

But an employee comes running out of the building. He opens my door and helps me out of the car.

"Mr. Burrows, your plane should be ready to depart in about twenty minutes. The crew is already here, going through all the usual safety checks and preparing the plane. Your assistant just arrived with your luggage. So, if you'll follow me, I'll take you to your luggage to ensure you have everything before you board," the man says to Sean, both men ignoring me.

I hold on to my cat as I follow the men into the building and then into another room where there are at least half a dozen suitcases on the floor. My eyes widen at the sight of so many suitcases, but none of them are mine. Maybe the three bright pink ones are supposed to be mine, but I don't own any suitcases like that.

"I'll give you a few moments to make sure you have everything you need before the flight," the man who still hasn't introduced himself to me says before leaving.

"You can change if you want, or you can stay in pajamas and change later on the plane. It really doesn't matter. Whatever makes you most comfortable," Sean says.

"I'm not sure your assistant went to the right apartment. These aren't my suitcases."

Sean rolls his eyes and then bends down. He opens the first suitcase, and it mostly contains my clothes. "She probably just used some new bags because yours weren't suitable."

I frown as I walk over and start digging through the suitcase to find a pair of jeans and a shirt to wear. "My suitcases were perfectly fine," I say angrily even though I know that's not the truth.

I own one duffel bag that has a decent-sized hole in it, and that's it. Nothing that even comes close to being called luggage by Sean's standards. But I don't want Sean to know that I have no money for things like suitcases.

I find some pants and shirts that aren't mine. "Some of these clothes aren't mine."

Sean shrugs. "My assistant might have picked up some additional clothes for you to wear."

I frown. "And why would she have done that? I thought this was going to be a short trip. Why do we need so many clothes?"

"I'm sure she just wanted to make sure you had plenty of options. Your regular clothes are fine."

I stand up and walk to the door to go find a restroom to change in. I'm not changing in front of him right now with him bossing me around and thinking my things aren't good enough.

"Watch my cat while I change," I say as I leave, hoping that my cat is just still breathing when I return.

I change quickly, feeling much more normal when I'm wearing actual clothes instead of pajamas. Back in the room, I put my pajamas into the suitcase while Sean stares at me. It takes me a second to notice, but he's cuddling my cat in his arms, gently stroking her head absentmindedly, while he stares at me. I walk over to him, giving him a small smile as I take the cat out of his arms.

"Well, I'm glad that at least Milo likes you."

Sean smiles.

"Are you ready to board the plane?" the employee from earlier asks as he pokes his head into the room.

"Yes," Sean says, looking over at me.

I nod slowly. Sean walks over and puts his hand on the small of my back, like I have found that he often does. He guides me out of the room and then out of the building to where I see a jet waiting for us.

I look from it and back to Sean. "Do you really own this plane?" I ask about the huge jet sitting in front of us.

Sean shrugs. "Yes, it's really mine. It's not a big deal. Really."

Owning a jet is a big deal, I think.

Sean leads me up the stairs and onto the plane. When we get on, I realize just how much of a big deal it really is. The plane is bigger than my apartment. I stop in the doorway, unable to move, not sure if I can handle going on a trip with someone who has a vastly different amount of wealth than me.

"What is it?" Sean asks.

"It's just so big."

Sean laughs. "I'm glad that size impresses you."

We both laugh as I walk further onto the plane. There are several regular chairs toward the front, followed by a small dining area, and then a door labeled *Bedroom* at the back. I turn back and look at Sean.

"No," he says before taking a seat in one of the chairs at the front.

I narrow my eyes at him as I take a seat next to him. I buckle my seat belt, just like he does. I put Milo down on the ground, letting him explore his new surroundings before we take off.

"What do you mean, no?"

"I mean, no. I can already tell what you're thinking. What your body is saying. You don't hide your feelings when it comes to what you want."

"And what do I want?" I whisper.

Sean grins. "You want me to take you to the back room, tie you up, and do something crazier than you've ever done before. Fuck you on this plane and make you feel things that only I can make you feel. That's what you want, but the answer is no."

I frown, hating his answer, but then maybe, once we're up in the air, I'll be able to convince him.

"No," Sean says again.

"What this time?" I ask.

"No. You aren't going to convince me. I don't care if you strip naked in front of me. I'm not going to fuck you on this plane."

I pout. *What good is it to be fucking your boss if you don't even get to fuck him on his private jet?*

Sean shakes his head. "I'll fuck you on the way back if you still want me to then."

I smile and sink back into the chair as the captain boards the plane, explaining all the safety features and how long it'll take to get to Vegas. Then, he enters the cockpit, leaving us alone in the back.

Vegas. We're going to Vegas.

I'm excited to be going to a city that I've never been to before. Even though Vegas isn't on the top of my list of places to visit, I'll take it. And I get to find out what Sean does for a living. Since we're going to Vegas, I have some pretty good guesses at what Sean does. He owns a casino, strip club, or hotel chain. It has to be something like that.

Our plane takes off, and I close my eyes, trying to rest since I won't be able to get Sean to fuck me on the plane. But then I look over at Sean, who is studying me with a worried expression on his face. I don't know what he has to worry about. He's a businessman who deals with what I'm sure is some level of shady business, just like every other millionaire on this earth. Whatever it is, it isn't going to make me change how I feel about him, and that's what scares me. I care about him a lot more than I should.

15

SEAN

OLIVE SLEPT the entire plane ride while I was a complete wreck. It's a feeling I rarely feel, and I don't plan on feeling it ever again. She slept calm and peacefully, not even realizing what her future holds. I know exactly what my future holds, and although I know it is for the best for both of us, I hate that I'll have to let her go so soon.

I was really a mess through the whole plane ride. I don't think Olive knew that, or if she did, she didn't let on. She just slept like an angel while I tried to ingrain her memory forever into my head. She probably thought it was helping us both to resist temptation if she slept, but all it did was make my desire for her worse. Ever since she gave me that look when she saw the bedroom on the plane, I've been going crazy, trying to keep my hands off her.

I'll admit that I've used the bedroom numerous times before. In fact, it's the main reason that I bought the plane. But I've never wanted to take a woman over my shoulder, carry her to the back of the plane, and fuck her. But fucking her wouldn't solve anything. I would just want to fuck her again and again and again and again. Because fucking her once didn't satisfy me.

Fucking her twice didn't satiate me. Fucking her three times will just make me want her more.

Thank God the stress of what I'm about to do will distract me from how much I want to fuck her. But I can't help but notice how beautiful and curious Olive is, riding in the car from the airport to my place. Her eyes are glued on all the shiny lights, buildings, and people as we turn onto the Vegas strip.

"Have you ever been to Vegas before?" I ask even though I already know the answer from how excited she is to see everything. It's clear she's never been here before.

"I've barely ever left the state of Illinois. The only other major trip I've taken was an eighth-grade field trip to Washington DC. I saved all my babysitting money for a year in order to go on the trip."

I suck in a breath. It makes it so much harder, and it is going to be so much more shocking to her when she finds out what I do. She is so innocent and pure. So different than what my life is.

Even though I know I should be distancing myself from her, I can't help but ask her, "If you could travel anywhere in the world, where would it be?"

"Everywhere," she says with a smile on her face.

It kind of shocks me that the girl that has barely ever left Chicago wants to travel everywhere, yet she hasn't. She hasn't traveled anywhere, not really, not on her own. It makes me more curious than ever as to why she's stayed with Jamie when it's clear that Jamie doesn't pay her what she's worth.

Yes, there are some leadership skills that Olive lacks, mainly the need for brutal honesty and forcefulness, but with a little nourishment, she's already shown that she can grow, and it's clear that she has the skills to be anything she wants.

So, again, I ask a question that I shouldn't want to know the answer to, "Why do you keep working for Jamie? It's clear you're destined for much greater things. Jamie doesn't even pay you what you're worth."

Olive's eyes drop as she thinks back to a memory that I'm afraid is much darker than I'm ready to hear. "Because she saved me, and I owe her."

I blink as I try to remember Jamie ever telling me about saving Olive, but I can't remember anything.

"Whatever she did for you isn't enough for you to stay in a job where you aren't growing."

"But it is," is all she says before turning her eyes back out into the bright lights.

She's clearly not going to tell me exactly what Jamie did to save her. That's okay. She doesn't have to tell me. I'll find out from Jamie. She tells me everything, and I know she'll tell me this as well.

We ride in silence while the lights get brighter and then finally softer as we turn from the excitement of the strip to the business area of town where I work and live. My driver pulls up in front of the tall building, and Olive's eyes immediately go up and down the huge skyscraper.

"Do you live or work here?" she asks.

"Both."

She looks back at the building, studying it, trying to figure out how I could do both.

"Most of the floors are offices or places where the business is run, except for the top floor. That is where my personal condo is. I like being close to my work."

The driver opens Olive's door, and she stares back at Milo, who is sound asleep between us.

"Leave him. I'll have my staff take him up and get him settled into my condo. I need to show you what I do first before we head up to my condo."

Olive nods, but I can finally see the hint of anxiety in her eyes. She is just as nervous to find out what I do as I am to tell her.

I climb out of the car and walk over to her side, linking my fingers with hers to hold her hand. It feels so good, holding her hand like this, most likely for the last time.

I lead her into the building and over to the elevator that opens automatically when I press the button. We walk inside, both anxious as we enter an elevator again. Both thinking about the last time we were in an elevator together, wishing that we could go back to that place, but we can't.

But I can bring one quick moment back. I kiss her one last time. Our lips connect as we ride up the three floors, and that's all it takes for our breathing to become even again, our hearts to stop beating so rapidly, and our world to be okay again. One kiss, and everything's okay again.

But, a second later, the elevator doors open, and I don't hesitate because I know, if I hesitate, I won't go through with it. I take her hand, and I pull her out of the elevator and into my world.

I look around as I see everyone walking around, staying busy and trying to make things happen. Today is a great time to take Olive here because she gets to see exactly what goes on here.

But I'm not here to ensure that everyone is working hard like they should be. I'm here to see how Olive reacts.

Her eyes grow large as she takes everything in. The amount of people in the room, the cameras, and then finally the naked people. I expect her quick, immediate response to be painful for me, but it's not how she reacts. She takes her time studying everything, taking it in and trying to understand.

"You make porn for a living?" she asks, slowly scanning the room, trying to make sense of it.

"Yes. I'm in the adult entertainment industry. I make porn movies, and I sell sex toys. My job is to sell sex."

She swallows and nods, like it all makes sense. "I figured you owned a strip club or something like this," she says.

I grab her chin and tilt her head toward me. "This isn't like owning a strip club. Stripping is nothing compared to this. I hire people to have sex in front of a camera in order for me to make millions."

She sucks in a breath as she looks at me. Then, she finally nods, but she's not running away yet. Maybe she's in shock.

I take her hand again and pull her toward the camera. Many people nod and smile and acknowledge me as we walk by. Most of my employees like me because I'm a fair boss, and they know exactly what I expect of them. I show up at work often, trying to be as involved as I can be. I try to make the working conditions the best they can be.

"Watch," I say as the director starts shooting another scene.

The scene the two actors are in is pretty tame compared to some of the things I've seen and produced.

They are supposed to be in a classroom. The woman is a teacher, and the man is supposed to be her student. The woman eventually seduces her student, and then they fuck on her desk. It's a good scene to ease Olive into this world. The actors truly enjoy what they do, and they want to be here. But that's not the same for everybody. I've seen too many actors come and do this just to make a quick buck and not because they love it, and it ends up destroying them.

I watch Olive's face as she watches them have sex in front of her. She blinks a lot as she watches. Her face occasionally flushes a slight shade of pink. But she doesn't turn away in disgust. She doesn't say that I'm degrading women or anything that I was expecting.

When the scene is over, I grab her hand and pull her out of there and into the side room that we use for interviews and meetings. I shut the door and flip on the lights so that I can see her. I need to know how she feels. Now.

"What do you think?" I ask.

"I think...I think...I don't know what to think. I don't like it. I don't understand it."

My heart sinks.

"But I don't hate it."

I can live with that, I think.

"And what do you think of me?" I ask, needing to know if she hates me.

She narrows her eyes at me. "I think I like you more than I should, more than what's good for me."

I grin even though I shouldn't. I get to keep Olive in my life for a little bit longer. She doesn't hate me...yet.

I grab her and spin us around while kissing her hard on the lips. When I put her down, I say, "I can't wait to fuck you in the bed on my plane."

She bashfully bites her lip, and then her eyes catch something in the corner of the room. She stops grinning. She stops paying any attention to me as she walks slowly over to the corner. I slowly turn around, but I already know what's in the corner of the room.

Everything I thought I had with her, the little time I thought I had left with her, is now gone.

I look at Olive looking at the DVDs of me on the front, shirtless, with words like, *Sean and Stacey in* College Facials. I knew that she wouldn't be happy when she found out that I not only produced porn, but I also starred in them. What's worse is, the other person on the covers of most of them—Jamie.

"Olive, I can explain..."

But I know I can't. There's nothing to explain. There's nothing to be sorry for. This is my life. This is what I do, and if she can't accept me, then I don't want her in my life.

Olive slowly turns around, and I see the tears rolling down her cheeks. "I need some air," she says, pushing past me and out of the room.

This is why I wanted to show her the real me—so she could run away. But, now that she has, I know that isn't what I wanted at all.

16

OLIVE

I WRAP my arms around myself because the cool night air hits me hard when I walk outside into the night. But I can finally breathe, alone in the dark. Except I'm not alone. I'm in a busy city full of people walking by who don't bother to stop and ask if I'm okay when they see the tears burning down my cheeks. I should be thinking about Sean, about who he is and what he does, but all I can think about is that I should've brought a damn jacket.

I pace up and down the sidewalk, trying to warm my body and figure out why I had the reaction that I just had. I shouldn't be upset that Sean owns and runs an adult entertainment company. I shouldn't be upset that he did or still stars in porn. I shouldn't be upset that he had sex with Jamie at least a dozen times on film for the world to see. I shouldn't be upset because he is not mine.

I don't have any claim to him, and I definitely don't have any claim to his past. For all I know, he's had sex with women in between our times together. But, still, the tears fall because it hurts to know how intimately involved Sean and Jamie were. They make sense together, unlike me and Sean. Jamie has always been strong, powerful, driven. She knows what she wants, and she goes after it, just like Sean. I don't understand why I feel so strongly about them.

No, that's not true. I know exactly why it makes me so upset.

One, because I care about Sean far more than I hate him.

Two, I know I'm the real reason that Jamie and Sean are no longer together.

It all comes back to me.

The endless nights of listening to Jamie talk about her baby, honey, sweetheart. It took me a while to connect the dots because she hardly ever used his real name when talking about him when they were together.

I try to push the thought out of my head, but I can't. I broke them up. I just didn't realize it at the time.

They were perfect for each other, and I ruined it. And, now, I'm making it worse by fucking Sean. Jamie will never be able to forgive me, and I can't handle being in any more of her debt.

How do I tell Sean the truth? How do I give him up? How can I fix this now that Jamie is pregnant with another man's baby?

I can't.

That's the only thing I know for sure. There is no way to fix this. What's done is done. I just have to figure out how to move on from this.

I take a deep breath and wipe my tears off on the back of my hand. I fluff my hair before I turn around and walk back inside the building. I don't take the elevator. I take the stairs, needing time to think as I climb each step.

I step out onto the floor where there's a whole crew of people shooting the film, not paying any attention to me. I scan the crowd, looking for Sean but don't immediately see him. I wander around on the floor, continuing to look for him while taking everything in.

"He's not here," a woman's voice says.

I turn around and realize that the woman is talking to me. She's beautiful with long, long blonde hair, and when I see the robe wrapped around her body, I realize instantly that she's the woman from the film.

"Who?" I ask.

"Sean. He's not here. That's who you are looking for. You're his new girlfriend."

"I'm not sure I would say that. More like his new plaything for a little while."

The woman laughs. "If you are just his plaything, then why did he bring you here? He hardly ever brings women here unless he's serious about them. It's one of his tests. And you're failing horribly."

I frown. "I know. But I didn't freak out because of what he does. It's more complicated than that."

She nods. "It always is."

"Where is he?"

The woman glances up, and I know immediately that he retreated to his condo.

"Thank you," I say. I run to the elevator and press the button for the top floor.

"You're going to need the code to access his floor," the woman says from behind me.

I feel in my pockets, but I don't have my cell phone to text him. It's with my personal belongings that I left in the car for Sean's staff to take up to the condo. I have no way to reach him. *Shit.*

The elevator doors open, but I don't know what to do because I can't reach him even if I step on. The woman steps on and starts entering a code into the panel. I step in behind her and try not to think about the reason she knows the code to access Sean's floor.

"Don't hurt him," she says as she steps off the elevator.

I frown. *Why does she think that I would hurt him?*

The doors close, and they don't open again until I reach the top floor.

When the doors open, I expect another obstacle in my way, preventing me from getting to Sean, but that's not the case. When the doors open, they open straight to his condo. And it's the most massive condo I think I've ever been inside of. His condo in Chicago isn't even half of the size of this place.

But I try not to focus on how massive and beautiful and expensive his place is. I try to focus on the man sitting on the couch with Milo in his lap and a drink on the end table as he stares out the window in silence.

I know that he knows I'm here because Milo's head pokes up, looking at me, and there's no way he didn't hear the elevator. But, still, I cautiously walk over and take a seat on the other end of the couch, tucking my feet under me. I prepare for a fight of some sort or a breakup to happen even though we were never really together. But he doesn't say anything to me. He just blankly looks at me, unfeeling.

"I don't know what to say," I say.

Sean takes a drink of his amber liquor and then says, "Tell me that you hate me."

He says what he wants me to say. I know that he brought me here to end whatever was going on between us. But it's not what he wants. He wants to be with me—or at least, he wants to fuck me again. I'm not sure if he really wants me. He probably wants to be with Jamie.

"I don't hate you. I wish I did. It would make everything easier," I whisper.

He nods.

I want to apologize. I want to find a way to fix things, but I can't. I know that's not what he wants anyway.

He just wants me to accept him for who he is. And I do, and I don't care what he does for a living. But it still doesn't mean that we can be together. I just don't know what it means yet.

I feel entirely exhausted and drained even though I slept for hours on the plane. I feel so tired. I'm tired because I didn't get much sleep the night before due to my migraine. I'm tired from dealing with Owen. I'm tired of trying to figure Sean out.

"What's my final test?" I ask, hoping that shows him that I still approve of him enough to be here.

He raises an eyebrow, surprised at my question. "You need to hire five actors tomorrow for a new film. The script is on the kitchen counter for you to read through."

"I'll read it before I go to sleep, which I need to do soon," I say, waiting to hear what he's going to say. I try not to think about the script that is basically just a sex scene that I'm somehow supposed to audition actors for. Instead, I think about the sleeping part. *Am I going to sleep in his bed? Am I going to sleep alone?* I don't have an answer.

"Like I said, the script is on the counter. You won't need to be ready until one tomorrow afternoon. That's when the auditions start. And you can take any of the rooms in this condo."

I suck in a breath because he's not making the decision of where I sleep tonight. I am. I can sleep in his bed if I want, or I can sleep on my own in any of the other beds.

I get up off the couch and walk over to the kitchen where I pick up the script. Then, I head down the long hallway. I pass door after door, each bedroom all more than acceptable rooms to sleep in. But I don't stop until I find the door on the end. When I open it, it looks just like his retreat in his Chicago condo.

I hesitate for a second, knowing that this is just going to make things even more complicated, but I don't care. I want to sleep with Sean tonight even if there's no chance we'll have a tomorrow. So, I walk into his bedroom, and then I wait.

17

SEAN

THAT WAS the first time that I slept in a bed without fucking a woman first. I probably could have. Olive probably even wanted me to with the way she was lying in my bed, sound asleep, when I came in. She'd climbed into my bed completely naked, and by the time I came in, the covers were halfway down her body, exposing her perfect breasts, begging me to touch them. But I was good—mainly because I didn't want to wake her up. She looked so peaceful, sleeping in my bed.

But, now, it's the next day, and I honestly have no idea where we stand. I thought that bringing her here would make everything clearer. I thought she would return to hating me like she did before, and that would be that. That, no matter how much I wanted to fuck her, she would say no every time, and I'd eventually give up and move on to another woman. But that's not what happened. Everything became more complicated.

My dick still wants her. Man, does he want her. I want her lips, her ass, her pussy. I want to push my dick inside every bit of her. *But do I want more than just to fuck her? Does she want more? I'm not sure. What would that even look like? How would we manage a relationship while working together?* And I'm still not sure she's okay with the fact that I sell sex for a living even if it's not my body I'm selling anymore.

And there is still a past between her and Jamie that I don't understand. I tried to get Jamie to tell me this morning when I called her. But she wouldn't tell me. That could be another complication. And, since Jamie won't tell me, I'll have to work on Olive telling me.

But, for now, I get to push that all aside and just enjoy the afternoon. Because, right now, it's time for Olive's final test. I've already decided that she's going to be my manager for me when I'm gone. She's the only person I trust, and she's already proven herself more than capable of handling any situation. I still want to do the test today because it's going to be a hell of a lot of fun to watch her be uncomfortable all afternoon while trying to pretend like she's not.

I hand Olive the stack of headshots of the actors. She takes them from me and places them on the table next to the script and her notebook that she has some things scribbled on. I'm guessing she has written interview questions and things like, *Remain calm*, and, *Don't stare at the guys' dicks too much*.

"This is your final test, so make sure you really prove to me that you're capable of leading and taking control of any situation," I say.

Olive rolls her eyes at me. "Don't act like you haven't already decided who's going to be the manager. I know I already have the job. And, if I don't, I'm suing you for sexual harassment," she says with a smile.

I grin as I look at her. Then, I lean down, so my lips hover just over her ear, and I whisper, "Cocky. I like it, but just remember how much I enjoy punishing you when you mess up, and remember that we're in a building full of all sorts of sex toys that you told me earlier you were afraid of. I could use far too many things in this building to punish you, and it would be far too enjoyable for me to make you so uncomfortable that you won't be able to walk straight for a week."

I take a seat in the chair at the table next to her as her eyes follow me. I see the hint of fear but also lust in her eyes at that thought.

I grin, happy to have made this challenge even harder for her. "Are you ready, Olive?" I ask.

She nods.

"We're ready for the first round of actors!" I shout out the door of the audition room.

One of my assistants opens the door and lets the first five actors in. I watch as Olive calmly folds her hands together and lays them on the table, watching the actors walk into the room.

"Can you please tell me your name, a little about yourself, and what your last project was?" Olive says politely to them.

I don't pay attention to the actors, just Olive. She listens with a bright smile on her face as each actor introduces themselves. She pulls out each headshot and résumé from the stack as they speak.

"I'll now have you act out the first scene," Olive says without an ounce of hesitation or fear in her voice.

I keep my eyes on her as actors get in position. But I can see them out of the corner of my eye, stripping most of their clothes off in order to prepare for the scene. The scene is much darker than what she saw yesterday. It's a gangbang. Four men, one woman. And I don't know how far she's gonna want them to take the scene for her to decide who the best people for this job are. There is not really a right or wrong answer, although I usually have them take it far enough that I can decide how well they work together, enough for them to get into the scene and make me believe them.

Honestly, I don't care if she picks all the wrong people for this next project. I just want to watch her grow uncomfortable and twist in her chair because I know watching her will drive me wild. I hear them start the scene with some seductive conversation. But Olive doesn't change her expression. She just calmly sits there, like she's watching an audition for a musical. The scene progresses, and I know that she is staring at guys holding their dicks as they prepare to fuck the actress.

But, still, Olive remains calm. Her eyes don't show any fear or anxiety. Her breathing is calm and relaxed, but there is one tiny thing that gives her away. Her heart. I brush my hand against her leg, and I can feel her pulse beating rapidly through her body.

I grin. She might be pretending to be calm, but this is driving her wild inside.

She stops the scene a minute later, and I glance over to see where she stopped it—the exact moment after each of the men have had a chance to interact with the girl. It's where I would have stopped them as well.

"Thank you all for coming. We will get back to you within the next couple of hours," Olive says, standing out of her chair and extending her hand. As she does, her chair falls backward, making a loud clash.

One of the men whom she's holding out her hand to, who is still standing completely naked and covered in sweat—among other things—says with a grin, "I don't think you want to shake my hand right now."

She retracts her hand. "You're probably right," she says, wincing. "It was nice to meet you all," she says, sitting back down after picking up her chair.

I can't help but laugh at her just a little.

She playfully punches me in the arm. "Stop laughing. You have to admit, I handled that pretty well, and I don't think I'm ever going to come across a situation like this ever again in my life."

I keep laughing because I can't help it until she gives me a serious look. I stop it as the next few actors come into the room.

The process repeats over and over again, but every time, I look to see if it still affects her. And, every time, her heart still races in her chest, and her blood still pumps quickly throughout her body, letting me know that, despite her cool exterior, the auditions are driving her wild.

The last actors finally leave, and then I ask, "So, who would you pick?"

She digs through the headshots and places the third group out on the table.

"This group. But, if I'm allowed to exchange some actors from different groups, then I'd replace this guy with this guy from the first group," she says, pointing to the various headshots.

I nod, entirely agreeing with her.

"Did I pass? Do I get the job?" she asks, crossing her arms and leaning back in the chair.

I scrunch my lips together, pretending to think about it for a couple of minutes, watching her frown, which in turn makes me laugh. "Yes, the job is yours. You're the only one I trust to be me when I'm gone."

She jumps up and throws her arms around me. She firmly kisses me on the lips, surprising us both.

"What was that for?" I ask when she slowly pulls away.

"Sorry. I guess watching people have sex all afternoon has made me a bit horny," she says, blushing for the first time all afternoon.

I laugh and then kiss her again, more than happy to remedy the situation.

My phone buzzes in my pocket for about the dozenth time this afternoon. I reluctantly pull it out and see text message after text message from Frank and the other employees back at Jamie's real estate company.

I sigh. "I think we'd better get back sooner rather than later. It seems the company is falling apart without us there."

Olive frowns.

"Don't worry; this time, we can actually fuck on the plane."

Her eyes light up at that thought. Then, she reaches over into her purse that is sitting on the floor next to her and pulls out a DVD with me and two women on the front, half-naked.

"And maybe we can watch this?" she says with a goofy grin on her face.

I laugh. And I nod.

I can't believe she did that. I think it's her way of showing me that she accepts me, no matter what I've done or what I still do for a living. And I don't know if I've ever wanted a woman more.

18
———

OLIVE

WE BARELY MAKE it back onto Sean's private jet before our lips lock, our hands clinging to each other without a thought of letting go.

"Mr. Burrows, you need to take a seat for us to take off," a man, who I assume is our captain, says.

Sean moves us further onto the plane.

"We'll be in a seat in the back," Sean says between kisses.

He starts pulling me down through the aisle of the plane. His hands travel over my body while his lips stay glued to mine.

I'm not sure if the captain is going to allow us to sit in the back. I'm sure he knows that we won't be sitting in the bedroom. But he doesn't say anything to us. I guess, when you own your own jet, it doesn't really matter if you follow all the rules.

And, right now, I want to break all the rules. Every. Single. One.

I want to feel things I have never felt before. Do things I have never done before.

I want to know what it is really like to be loved by a man who truly loves me. I'm just not sure if Sean is the man I will get to experience real love with. But I do know that I get to experience the best sex of my life with him.

Sean pulls me into the bedroom and slams the door shut behind us.

"I want it dirty. Show me how dirty and rough you can be, just like in the videos you make," I say.

Sean stops kissing me long enough to cock his head to one side with a look I haven't seen before. "I don't think you understand how dirty it can really get."

I grin. "I think I've seen plenty dirty so far. But I want more."

Sean kisses me hard. "Tell me what you want, Olive."

I bite my lip as I think about what I want. "Tie me up, spank me, talk dirty to me. I want everything."

Sean's eyes intensify.

"Show me how to fuck like a porn star," I say.

He grabs my arm and forces it behind my back, and then he pulls the other one behind my back as well. "You like it rough, you'll get it rough, baby," Sean says.

He ties my hands together behind my back with rope that I have no idea where he got it from.

"I knew you would want it rough, so I brought some things with me," Sean whispers into my ear, answering my unspoken question.

He spins me around to face him and then rips my shirt open, exposing my lace bra that I found packed in my suitcase, which one of Sean's staff must have bought for me. It's more expensive than anything I own, and it makes my breasts look amazing. From Sean's gaze, I think he agrees.

But then he rips the thin material holding my bra in place. "My dirty girl thinks she needs to wear lace to impress me, but I'd rather just have you naked."

I suck in a breath as his tongue travels down my body and then over my breasts, teasing me in a way that only he can.

"I need you," I say. But I don't know what I need. All I know is that I need more. I'm consumed by need for him, and I'm not sure that I will ever get enough.

He rips my pants off my body and then throws me on the bed. I've never been so turned on as I am right now. The excitement of not knowing how far he is going to take it, how dirty it is going to get, is driving me mad with need.

I feel his palm hit against my bare ass, and I scream from the shock. Then, I realize that we are on a plane that, albeit is huge, is not huge enough to hide my screams.

Sean grins. "You can scream, baby. This room is just as soundproof as any of my bedrooms."

His hand hits my ass again, and I scream again. The pain is more than I expected, especially since I can't move. My hands are tied behind my back, my face is smushed into the bed, and my ass is up in the air.

He hits me again, and I cry out, but as much as I don't want to admit it, being controlled like this turns me on even more.

"You like it like this. Dirty, filthy," Sean says.

I pant. "Yes."

I feel the sting on my ass again.

Then, he says, "I want to fuck your ass. I want you to feel what it's really like to feel dirty. I want to claim every last bit of you."

I suck in a breath. Liking and hating that thought at the same time.

I feel his cock already pushing at my ass, begging to enter.

I feel him tug on my hair, pulling my head up as he kisses down my neck.

"Tell me you want me to fuck your ass."

He kisses my neck as his hand finds my pussy. His fingers rub over me until his hands are soaked with my wetness. His fingers move the wetness from my pussy to my ass. He gently slides his finger in my ass, and I moan as he stretches me.

"I want you to fuck me in the ass," I say, barely able to get the words out because it feels so good.

He slaps my ass again just as his cock replaces his fingers.

I forgot how large he was until he pushed inside my ass.

He slaps me again as he thrusts inside me.

I scream, "Fuck, Sean."

He kisses my lips. "That's my dirty girl."

I nod, loving being his dirty girl. If only I were really his. If this is how he fucks me now, I would love to know what it would be like for him to fuck me when and if he actually made me his.

But thoughts like that easily leave my mind when he fucks me harder. Pounding into me until I can't take it any longer.

I come as he fills my ass with his own cum.

He cuts the rope off my wrists and then wraps his arms around me as he sweetly kisses my neck.

I suck in a breath, letting the emotions I feel run through me.

"I lo—" I begin but then stop myself.

"Hmm?" Sean says, barely awake.

I shake my head as I continue to breathe heavily. "I think I like being your dirty girl."

He softly kisses me on the lips and pulls me tighter to him. I know, within seconds, we are both going to be sound asleep.

But I can't help but think that I could love him. I might even already be in love with him.

I just need to stop loving him. He's my boss, and he's made it perfectly clear that he is in love with Jamie, not me.

This was a last fling, and I just got carried away. I don't love him.

19

SEAN

I COULD HEAR it in Olive's voice. She has something else she wants to tell me, but she's hiding it from me. So, while she thinks I'm sleeping, I'm doing anything but. Instead, I'm reliving every last second, trying to figure out what she could be hiding and wondering if it's the same thing that I'm hiding.

Olive's eyes flutter open, and then a slow grin creeps up her face.

"I love naked naps with you," she says, her cheeks bright and flushed with warmth from her nap.

I stroke a piece of hair out of the way of her face as I continue to hold her in my arms.

She smiles brighter and stretches her arms above her head before snuggling her head against my chest again. "How much longer is left in our flight? I need to know when I should start getting dressed again, so it doesn't look like we just fucked the whole flight."

"Half an hour," I say.

"Oh. I should get up then and start looking presentable," she says, moving out of my arms to go get dressed.

I grab her arm and pull her back into bed.

She giggles. "Fine. I guess we can fuck one last time. But we have to make it quick." She moves to kiss me but stops short when she sees the look in my eyes. "What is it?" she asks.

I take a deep breath as I tuck her messy brown hair behind her ear again. "I think I might just fall in love with you if given the chance."

She sucks in a breath and then stops breathing altogether.

"Say something," I say, needing to know how she feels.

But she doesn't. She doesn't even breathe.

"Olive, say something. Anything."

She doesn't.

I grab her cheeks, pulling her face toward mine, and kiss her, sweeping my tongue into her mouth.

When I pull away, she finally breathes again, coming to after I kissed her.

"Say something."

"I..." She grins.

I cock my head as I wait, second after second, for her to finish her sentence. My heart beats fast as I wait the unbearable seconds.

"I think I already love you."

My lips crash down on hers as my hands cling to her body. Now, I need to fuck her again.

She laughs. "Wait...I love you, and it's clear you love me even if you won't fully admit it yet. But what does that mean? How will this work? We work together. You're still in love with..." But she doesn't finish her sentence.

I grab her chin and look her square in the eye. "I'm in love with you."

Her eyes flitter back and forth between mine, trying to find the truth. But I'm not hiding anything. I'm telling her the truth.

When she's satisfied, she says, "And what about at work? The realtors aren't going to be happy with us dating and my promotion."

I nod. "They don't have to know that we are dating."

She narrows her eyes. "How? I can't keep a secret from the company for more than a couple of hours. I'm sure they have already figured out that I broke up with Owen, and they probably already know that I'm here with you, that we are together. We can't hide it from them."

"They have probably figured out that you broke up with Owen. But, as far as they know, you and I still hate each other. And I'll just say, I brought you here for training, which is the truth."

She nods, but I don't think I've convinced her.

"We will go to work and pretend to hate each other, as always. Then, at night, we will be free to do as we please. I can take you on fancy dates. Do more unthinkable things to your body."

Her breathing slows again.

"It will be fun, sneaking around the office, trying not to get caught," I whisper into her ear.

She bites her lip, and I know I have her.

"Now, come here, and let me fuck you before we land."

She squeals as I grab her.

Olive is mine.

"What the hell is going on?" I ask Floyd as I get back to the office.

Olive walks into the office past me and straight to her desk, practically ignoring me.

She's good, I think.

"We lost the Margo account. They were our biggest client.

We helped them find properties for their businesses and homes all over the world," Floyd says.

"How in the world did that happen?" I ask, not understanding how, in less than twenty-four hours, everything has fallen apart so horribly.

Floyd looks down. "We missed a few deadlines and weren't able to find them what they were looking for. They were already on thin ice before when we couldn't negotiate a lower price for a restaurant they opened last month."

I run my hand through my hair, not ready to deal with this now.

"You're fired," I tell Floyd.

"What? You can't do that! I'm the best realtor you have," Floyd says.

I shake my head. "No. You used to be the best realtor until you lost the most important account we had. Honestly, the only account that mattered since they made up almost sixty percent of our profit each year."

Floyd still stands there, stunned.

But I don't have time to deal with him. I brush past him and head straight toward my office, walking past Olive's desk.

"Olive, I need to see you. Now," I say with an angry voice.

I feel everyone's eyes on us as Olive stands up and follows me into my office. I glance behind Olive to see the employees looking on with fear instead of suspicion over Olive and me.

This is going to be too easy.

Olive shuts the door. "We lost the Margo account? We have to fix this! If Jamie finds out, it's going to destroy her. She's worked too hard for this company to lose everything in a few days," she says.

I nod. "I'm going to go speak with the CEO of Margo Enterprises in person and see if I can get things straightened out. I need you to keep everything running smoothly here for the rest of our accounts. We can't afford to lose anyone else."

I start gathering my things to leave. "What are you doing? Get to work!" I shout, letting my anger get the best of me.

Olive folds her arms across her chest and raises an eyebrow at me.

"I'm sorry. Olive, can you please get to work and help me straighten everything out? I don't want to ruin Jamie's company any more than you do."

She grins.

I cock my head to one side. "What?"

"I just never thought I'd hear you say *I'm sorry*."

I roll my eyes. "I guess there is a first time for everything."

"I'll help you...under one condition."

"What's that?"

"You kiss me first. And promise to come to my apartment after work tonight."

I grin. "I'll do everything I can to get to your bed as quickly as I can."

Her eyes light up.

I walk over to her, take her in my arms, and kiss her with everything I have. I forget about how much I'm screwing up by letting down one of my closest friends by basically ruining her company. I just kiss Olive until we hear a knock at the door.

I quickly let go of Olive and walk to the door while Olive stands, frozen.

"Yes?" I snap as I open the door.

"Here are my keys to the properties I was selling. I hope the whole company goes down in flames," Floyd says, throwing his keys at me.

He turns and leaves. Olive pushes past me and walks out after him.

She's mad at me. I can tell.

For firing Floyd? For yelling at her?

I'm not sure. I run my hand through my hair again and then rub my neck. I don't have time to figure it out now. I have a company to save.

I flash her a we-will-talk-later-and-we-are-still-on-for-fucking-at-your-place-tonight look as I walk by her desk, but she doesn't even glance up at me. Working with Olive is going to be harder than I thought.

20

OLIVE

SEAN NEVER MADE it to my apartment last night. He stayed at Margo's hotel, speaking with her employees most of the night, working out a new contract with them.

But he did call to apologize. Twice.

And I'm beginning to love hearing him apologize.

I can't wait to get into work today. Because it means that I will get to see Sean again. And, hopefully, now that the Margo account has been settled, we can get back into a normal swing of work, which will involve lots of sneaking around in his office to have sex.

So, I jump out of bed thirty minutes before my alarm even goes off, far too excited to get into work today. I jump in and out of the shower even faster. I throw on some clothes, but when it comes to doing my hair and makeup, I take a little more time then usual.

I want Sean to find me irresistible. I want him to not be able to think straight because all he can think about is me.

Milo brushes up against me while I finish applying my makeup. I pet him, giving him the attention he wants.

My phone buzzes, and I see the message is from Sean. I

smile as I open the text message, and immediately, my heart sinks.

Sean: I have to go to NYC for a week. Margo wants me to personally find her new property there to assure her that we can honor our new contract.

I frown. I don't get to see him today. I don't get to kiss him.

Is he running away from me?

I immediately push the thought out of my head. He's not running away at the thought of a serious relationship with me. He's not hiding. He's just working, doing what's right.

Still, it doesn't keep me from feeling horrible. I wish I could see him again before he goes.

It's a silly thought. I just saw him yesterday. There is no need to be so needy.

I take a deep breath trying to keep from letting the thought of him not being at work today make me fall apart. It's probably better actually that he won't be at work today. It will help keep people from getting suspicious about our relationship and it will allow me to start being respected as a leader without him here.

I text back.

Me: I'm going to miss you. Good luck!

He doesn't respond immediately. I try to distract myself by finishing getting ready, but that is no longer a distraction for me. I no longer care about what I look like when I get into work or getting in early.

I sulk while I finish getting ready. I do my best to take my time now that I don't have Sean to look forward to. But I quickly run out of things to do at home. I might as well get into work early. It will at least distract me.

I head downstairs. I decide to call an Uber when I see more than a foot of snow covering the ground. Sean and I never discussed what my new salary would be, but it has to be enough for me to at least afford an occasional Uber ride to work instead of taking the subway every morning.

I wait in the lobby until the Uber pulls up, and then I step out into the cold air, happy that I have the new coat that Sean bought for me to keep me warm and remind me of him on a day like today.

"You didn't think I would leave without saying good-bye first, did you?" I hear Sean's voice cut through the cool air.

I grin and turn around to see Sean walking toward me.

I run over to him, throwing myself in his arms like I haven't seen him in months instead of only hours. He catches me and wraps his arms around me like he is just as desperate for me as I am for him.

He firmly kisses me over and over, turning the kiss into a longer make-out session.

I slowly pull away. "You are full of surprises," I say.

Sean smiles and then walks me over to one of two cars parked along the street.

"Your chariot, fully stocked with coffee and chocolate chip cookies to get you through your day," Sean says.

"You got me a ride into work today?" I ask.

He nods.

I light up. "Oh, crap. I need to cancel my Uber then." I pull out my phone and quickly cancel it.

"You're going to do great today," Sean says, sweetly kissing me on the lips.

"Thank you," I say, blushing, still amazed that he is here and that he did all of this for me.

"This is Joe Hubbert. He'll be giving you a ride every day while I'm away," Sean says.

I smile and shake Joe's hand before turning back to Sean.

"And what about when you return?" I ask.

Sean kisses me again. "Since you'll be waking up in the same bed as me, I can give you a ride to work."

I bite my lip, trying to contain my excitement at that thought.

He groans as I kiss him again. "I really need to go."

I grab his neck and kiss him again. "Are you sure?"

He groans again. "No. But, if I'm going to make my flight, I have to go."

"You're flying commercial?"

He nods. "I'm reserving my private jet for flights with you. Otherwise, what is the point?" he says, winking.

"All right, get out of here. I'll keep you updated about how the realtors are doing."

He kisses me one last time. "I just want to hear how you are doing."

I nod. "Same."

He smiles and helps me into the car before shutting my door. Joe starts driving me toward work and away from Sean. Sean waits a second to watch me leave and then jumps in his car behind me before speeding off toward the airport.

———

That's the last I saw of him in over a week.

He calls to talk to me every day, usually multiple times a day, but it's still hard to have a real relationship with him when he's gone. It's why I have been looking forward to him coming back at the end of the week.

But, when Friday comes around, he calls to tell me it would be at least another week.

The thoughts of him running away from me immediately creep back into my head. Until he tells me he loves me and sends me a large bouquet of flowers to my desk at work. He didn't sign it with his name, just *Your love.*

But it is enough to get me through another week.

But, when the second week passes, I almost expect him to call again, saying that he isn't coming home for another week. But, to my relief, he says he is coming home tonight. I just have to make it through one more day at work, and then I'll get to see him.

Work has actually been great the last couple of weeks. I have loved being in my new role as manager. I passed my realtor's license test. I have made dozens of cookies for clients this week. My week has been great. The only downside has been not seeing Sean.

But, when I get into work on Friday morning, I'm afraid my luck has changed. Because sitting in the office when I first get in is Jamie. She's crying, sitting at what used to be her desk.

"Oh, thank God you are the first one here, like always, Olive," Jamie cries out.

I walk into Jamie's office and close the door behind me in case anyone else comes in.

"What's going on, Jamie? I thought you were supposed to be on bed rest?" I ask as I walk over to her and tightly hug her.

Jamie continues to cry as I hold her in my arms.

"Nicolas broke up with me," Jamie finally gets out through sobs.

"Oh, sweetie! I'm so sorry," I say, holding her tighter.

I don't know what to say to make it any better for her. She only dated Nicolas two months before she found out she was pregnant. I'm not sure what she expected. But I know telling her that now isn't helpful.

"Are you okay to be out of bed?" I ask.

Jamie nods. "The doctor said I was fine as long as I take things easy. I was just too stressed at work. But, right now, I need some sort of distraction."

I hold on to her. "Why don't I take you to brunch? Food

always makes you feel better, and then you can tell me every-thing that happened."

Jamie nods. "That sounds good. Sean is supposed to be back soon, and he can handle things here for us."

I smile. I'm not sure what Sean has told her about me and him. But it hurts me that Sean still talks to her so often, knowing their history. Knowing that they used to work together. Sleep together.

I stand up. "Let me just check in with everyone here first, and then we can go."

Jamie nods.

But, when I stand up, I feel off. I feel dizzy, sick, like I'm about to puke.

I close my eyes and sit back down on the ground to try to make the nausea and dizziness go away, assuming that I just stood up too fast. But it doesn't immediately go away.

"Olive, are you okay?" Jamie asks.

I nod and stand up again, but the feeling intensifies.

"Sorry, no, I'm not okay. I feel sick. Maybe I'm coming down with the flu. I'm sorry, Jamie, but I'm not sure if I can go to brunch with you after all."

Jamie studies me a moment and then says, "You're pregnant." She doesn't ask it. She says it.

I laugh. "You're crazy. I'm not pregnant. I'm just sick. The flu has been going around here lately."

Jamie shakes her head. "I could be wrong. It could be just because I'm pregnant that I expect everyone else to be, too. But humor me, and let's go get you a pregnancy test."

I frown, not understanding at all what is leading her to think I'm pregnant. I look down at the outfit I chose, and then I realize why. I chose a tight-fitting sweater that makes my pooch of a belly stick out just enough for Jamie to think that. I look bigger than Jamie does. Her belly still looks completely flat to me. She works out a lot, which I guess explains it.

"Please...at the very least, it will distract me," Jamie says.

"And what if I'm really sick with the flu? You think hanging out with me while you're pregnant is a good idea?"

She huffs. "You're right. How about you run to the drugstore next door and then come back here and take the test? If it's negative, then I'll keep my distance, but if it's positive..." Jamie lets her sentence trail off.

I sigh. "Fine," I say, realizing that Jamie isn't going to let this go.

I open the door and go grab my coat. Then, I head outside to walk the half a block to the drugstore to get a pregnancy test that I know is going to be negative.

I enter the drugstore a couple minutes later and easily find the pregnancy tests. There are about a dozen different brands though, and I have no idea which to choose. So, I just grab the cheapest brand, and then I walk over to the cold-and-flu section and pick up some meds because that is the more likely reason for me feeling so bad. I debate on picking up soup, but I can order delivery later. I'd rather have that than the cans of soup the drugstore carries.

I pay for the items and then walk back to the office through the freezing cold. *I can't believe I went outside and dealt with the cold just for a freakin' pregnancy test.*

When I get back to the office, more employees have arrived. I nod and greet them as I walk through the office building, trying my best to hide the contents of my bag. I don't want any rumors started about me, especially since I know I'm not pregnant.

I make it back to the office and slam Jamie's door shut.

"Did you get the pregnancy test?" Jamie asks.

"Shh. I don't want the whole office to know. And, yes."

"Well, what are you waiting for? Go take it."

I sigh and take the box out of the bag. I quickly read the instructions, not really paying that close attention, as I pull one of the tests out of the box and slip it into my purse. I then put the box back in the bag and hide the bag in the corner of the room in case anyone comes into Jamie's office while I'm gone.

"I'll be right back," I say.

"Good luck!" Jamie shouts at me as I leave.

I sigh. I don't need luck. I'm not pregnant.

I walk to the restroom on the third floor that no one from the real estate office ever uses just in case. The restrooms on this floor are single stalls, so when I enter, I lock the door and don't have to worry about anyone coming in.

I open the test and pee on the stick, and then I wait. I have to wait three minutes for the results. I set a timer on my phone.

I feel my heart begin to race as the seconds tick by. I wasn't nervous before, but I'm nervous now. This is ridiculous. I'm only taking this test because Jamie thinks she has a pregnancy sixth sense now that she is pregnant. I'm not pregnant.

Sean and I use condoms every time we have sex. Plus, it would be far too soon to know if I was pregnant.

The timer finally goes off, and then I remember. Owen. I could be pregnant with Owen's baby.

I stare at the test, unable to flip it over and read it.

"This is ridiculous! I'm not pregnant."

I walk over to the sink where the test rests and flip it over.

———

I walk back into the office to go tell Jamie the news when I freeze.

I watch as Sean hugs Jamie. It's clear that Jamie is telling Sean about how Nicolas broke up with her. Sean wraps his arm around her and tightly holds her as they walk into her office together. I watch Sean close the door but not before he gives her a look that I've only seen once before—when he told me he loved me. It's the same look he's giving her now.

He still loves Jamie.

The door shuts, but he slams it too hard, and it bounces open just slightly.

I don't know what to do.

Should I just walk in like I didn't know that Sean returned?

Should I just leave and not speak to either of them?

Should I just wait until one of them comes out of the office?

I still haven't decided. But, still, I walk toward the office and hesitate just outside the door.

I hear Sean's voice. "I'm so sorry, Jamie. I want to take care of you. I'll do anything for you and the baby. You know that."

I can't hear this. It will destroy me.

I turn to walk away when Jamie spots me through the small crack in the door.

"Olive!" she says brightly.

I open the door and step into the office. Sean doesn't immediately run over and hug me, like I expected. In fact, he stands, frozen, cold. Like he barely even knows me. Not like a man who is in love with me and has fucked me half a dozen times or more.

"Sean got back early, so we can go to brunch now, if you're feeling up to it," Jamie says.

Sean looks to me. "Are you sick?"

"No, I'm fine. I'd love to go to brunch with you, Jamie."

Jamie's face lights up when she realizes what it means.

"Oh my God! I was right then?" Jamie squeals.

I try to smile, but it's hard to smile. I nod slowly.

Jamie runs over and tightly hugs me. "I'm so excited for you!" she squeals.

I glance over at Sean, who is suspiciously staring at me.

Jamie finally releases her hold on me.

"What are we excited about?" Sean asks, looking from me to Jamie, trying to get one of us to give him an answer.

"Oh, nothing. I'm just excited to go to lunch with a good friend. Nothing you need to worry about," Jamie says, trying to protect my secret.

But I can't hold it in any longer. He needs to know the truth. Now.

I plaster a fake smile on my face. "I'm pregnant."

21
_____

SEAN

Pregnant.

Olive can't be pregnant. We haven't been having sex long enough for her to know if she is pregnant or not.

But then, all at once, it hits me. Owen. She's pregnant with Owen's baby.

I can see the fear in her eyes as she pretends to be excited with Jamie about being pregnant.

"I'm so excited for you and Owen. I know he isn't the perfect guy, but you two will make great-looking babies! And we get to experience this together! It's amazing!" Jamie continues on and on.

I can see the moment that Olive just can't take hearing Jamie any longer.

"I think I'm going to be sick. Can I take a rain check until a bit later, Jamie?" Olive asks.

"Oh, honey! Of course. I'll send you all my morning-sickness tricks," Jamie says.

That's all it takes for Olive to run out of the room.

"I'm going to go check on Olive," I tell Jamie.

"That's sweet, but you should just get her some Sprite and crackers for when she gets back," Jamie says.

I ignore her and chase Olive down the hallway to the restroom. She goes inside, and I follow her. I lock the door behind us.

"What are you doing? This is the woman's restroom," Olive says.

"And you aren't really sick. So, what are you doing in here?"

Her eyes slowly look up to mine. "I'm running away."

I walk toward her, needing to put my arms around her, but she takes a step back.

"I'm sorry that I ignored you back there, but I wasn't sure if you wanted Jamie to know about us," I say.

She folds her arms across her chest. "I'm not mad that you acted cold toward me back in Jamie's office. I understand. I really do. I just think we need to stop whatever this is. It doesn't make sense anymore."

I feel like she just slapped me.

"Why? Because you're pregnant?" I ask.

She nods. "I'm pregnant, and you already know it's not yours."

I rub my neck, trying to find the words to defuse the situation. "Yes, I know the baby isn't mine. But that doesn't matter. We can still date. Still see where this goes. And, no matter what happens, I will always be here for you and your baby."

"Like you are going to be there for Jamie?" she says solemnly.

"Yes," I say slowly, not understanding.

"I think you should just be there for Jamie and not for me. I have plenty of things to worry about without having to worry about where you and I stand."

"What are you talking about? I don't want Jamie. I want you."

She shakes her head. "You still love Jamie."

I frown but don't have any words to fix this. I can tell her that I don't love Jamie, but it is clear that she wouldn't believe me.

"I don't want to give you up," I say.

I see the tears starting, but Olive shakes them away.

"I broke you and Jamie up," she says almost defiantly.

"What are you talking about?"

"About five years ago, I was homeless. I was living on the street. Occasionally, I would get to sleep in a homeless shelter, but I mostly slept on benches in parks, tucked in the doorways of shops, or under highways.

"One night, I fell asleep on the doorstep of Jamie's small office. She only had two employees at that time. She had to wake me up to get into her office that day. She was running late, as always, so she asked me if I would get her a coffee. She offered to pay me ten bucks if did it, so I did.

"And then, the next morning, I got her coffee again. Eventually, she started paying me to be her assistant. She got me off the street and into the apartment that I live in now. She saved me.

"And so, a year ago, she told me about you. Except she never used your name. She always referred to you as her baby, honey, sweetheart, et cetera. She was so in love—or so she said. She thought you were going to propose soon. She was living the fairy-tale life.

"But, over the next couple of years, I got to know Jamie. I knew that, even though you had dated on and off for years, she wasn't ready to settle down. She had a company to run, and all she talked about was, once you proposed, she would sell the company and be a stay-at-home mom. But she wasn't ready for that. And, from everything I'd heard about you, you weren't ready for that. So..."

"So, you broke us up," I finish for her.

She nods.

"You showed her that message," I say.

She nods. "You left your phone at her apartment. So, I just let her see what an ass you were."

"She broke up with me because she thought I was cheating on her. But I wasn't."

The tears fall now. "I didn't realize it until later—when your mother texted that she loved you back. I hadn't realized it was your mother, but by then, Jamie had already broken up with you, and I thought it was for the best. I thought I was saving her from a life of unhappiness. I didn't want her to give up every-thing she had worked so hard for. She needed a man who fit into her life.

"I was one of her closest friends, yet the guy she had been seeing for over a year never even made an attempt to meet me. He never came to her work. She spent most of her time traveling to see him. I didn't think it was the healthiest relationship."

She takes a deep breath.

"But, now that I see you two together, I realize how mistaken I was. You two are perfect for each other."

Her tears flow freely while I'm in a state of shock.

"I'm so sorry, Sean," Olive says before she pushes past me, leaving me feeling completely empty.

My heart is broken. And I have no idea how to put it back together.

22

OLIVE

I quit.

I'd been calling in sick all week long, and tonight, I finally quit. Jamie invited me over to her house to get some maternity clothes that she said were too small for her, although I can't imagine them ever fitting me. And I told her that I was quitting.

She was sad but understood. I told her I was moving in with Owen, but I'm not sure she bought that. Honestly, I haven't even talked to Owen yet. I've been completely avoiding it like the plague.

Jamie wanted me to stay and talk about it, but I couldn't. I couldn't handle the thought that Sean could come over to her place at any moment or text or call her. Jamie was clearly back to her happy and bubbly self, so I'm guessing that she and Sean are back together.

I take a brownie from the tray I made earlier today and take a seat on my bed to eat it. Other than talking to Jamie, the only thing I've accomplished all week is baking and then eating everything that I baked. At this rate, I'll gain a hundred pounds in a month.

That can't be good for the baby. I should start making some avocado brownies or something, so at least, I will be getting something other than sugar into me.

I sigh.

I'm pregnant, I think, looking down at my stomach.

It's something I've always said I wanted but not this way with a man I hate. Although I've always wanted to be a mother, thinking about the fact that it is actually happening right now scares me to death.

Because, right now, if you asked me if I wanted a baby, the answer would be no. And that is a horrible thought.

I need to do something. Plan my life. Maybe then I'll feel better. If I have a plan for my life. A job. I need to find a new job ASAP if I don't want to end up back on the street.

It's too big to figure out right now. I don't know what I'm going to do. I have my real estate license. Maybe I could find a job with a new company or start my own. I have skills now. I'll find something to do.

There is something I need to do that I've been putting off all week. I need to tell Owen. He deserves to know. As much as I never want to see him again, I no longer have that choice.

I finish my brownie. Then, I get out of bed and get an Uber to Owen's apartment.

———

I've paced in front of Owen's door a dozen times now. I've lifted my hand several times to knock, but I've come short every single time.

Sean was wrong. He used to tell me that he thought I was brave and strong. But I don't have a brave or strong bone in my body right now.

I stand in front of Owen's door again. I raise my hand, and then the door suddenly opens.

"What the hell are you doing, Olive? I'm about to call the police," Owen says.

"I'm sor—" But I stop myself before I apologize because I'm not sorry. Not at all. "Can I come in?"

Owen raises an eyebrow. "Why would I let you in after you destroyed my property last time?"

I fold my arms across my chest. "We need to talk. So, either let me in or go to a coffee shop or something with me so that we can talk."

"I have nothing else to say to you," Owen says, trying to shut the door in my face.

"I'm pregnant!" I shout at the last minute.

The door slowly creeps back open, and Owen stares at me with narrow eyes. "And how is this my problem?"

I close my eyes, trying to remain calm and be the bigger person. "Because I thought you might want to know that it's yours."

He laughs like it is the most ridiculous thing he has ever heard. "How do I know it's mine? You've been with who knows how many men since me, and you were probably cheating with who knows how many men. It could be anyone's."

My mouth drops a little at the shock of what he said. Of all the ways I imagined this conversation going, I didn't imagine it going like this.

"The baby is yours."

He laughs again. "I don't believe you." He starts to close the door again and says, "Don't come back here again unless you are bringing brownies. That was the only thing you were ever good at anyway."

He slams the door shut in my face while I'm frozen at the door.

I'm on my own. Owen doesn't care. And I don't know if that makes me incredibly happy or incredibly sad. I'm happy that I don't ever have to see Owen again, but I'm incredibly sad that my child will grow up without a father. I know the feeling.

But I do have to thank Owen for one thing. He just gave me an incredible idea and the motivation to make it happen.

23

SEAN

"WHAT IS GOING ON?" Jamie asks. "You're falling completely apart on me. Do I need to come into work to help you out for a bit?"

"No. You need to stay right here on this couch, relaxing, like the doctor told you to," I say as I rub her feet on my lap.

"I don't know if I can. I thought I was leaving my company in the hands of the best two people in the world, but one quit on me, and the other one is falling apart," Jamie teases.

"What do you mean, one quit?"

"Olive quit. I've been expecting it for some time. Real estate and management have never been right for her. It's one of the reasons I never gave her a raise. I was hoping it would motivate her enough to find something else."

"That's not fair. Olive would have made a great manager," I say.

"I know that she would have. She just wouldn't have been happy. She needs to find something that truly makes her happy on her own."

"Olive never left before because she felt like she owed you. She was trying to be loyal to you."

Jamie bites her lip as she thinks for a moment. "You might be right. But it all worked out in the end. I think the thought of having a baby finally pushed her to find something that truly makes her happy."

I nod. I wasn't sure that Olive would leave. I thought she might stay and ask to open an office to run somewhere else. But she's gone. And I can't decide if it makes my life easier or harder.

"You're tickling me," Jamie says, laughing, pulling her feet out of my lap.

"Sorry," I say, looking at her again.

"Stop looking at me like that. You are freaking me out," Jamie says.

"Have you ever thought about us getting together again?"

Jamie frowns and sits up on the couch with her feet on the floor. "Why would I think about that?"

"Olive told me about what happened when we broke up. That it was all just a big misunderstanding. I didn't really cheat on you."

Jamie bites her lip. "I knew you didn't cheat on me."

"You mean, Olive told you?"

"No, I mean, I knew when she showed me that message that it was from your mom."

"I don't understand. Then, why did you break up with me?"

"Because I wanted the white picket fence, the house, the baby. And you didn't."

I frown. "I did, too. I always told you that I wanted to settle down, start a family, and have a normal life."

Jamie sighs. "Yes, you always told me that, but it isn't what you wanted."

I shake my head. "It is what I wanted. It's still what I want."

Jamie laughs. "I know you, Sean Burrows, better than you know yourself. You don't want a suburban house, and you don't want kids. I'm not even sure if you want a wife. You want adventure. You want someone who challenges you. You don't want to settle down."

"You're wrong."

Jamie sighs. "Then, tell me what you really want." She folds her hands in her lap and gives me her full attention, like that is going to make me change my mind about how I feel.

I open my mouth, but then I close it because I don't know.

"Tell me you want to fuck a hot blonde. Tell me you want a threesome. Tell me you want to travel the world and meet every woman you can in every city."

"I can't."

She rolls her eyes. "I'm right about this, Sean."

Her phone buzzes, and she picks it up to read the text message she got.

"Is that from Olive?" I ask.

Jamie starts typing into her phone, responding to the message. "No."

I frown and sink back into the couch, wanting to hear any news about what Olive is doing now. *How is the baby doing? Did she take Owen back?*

A slow smile creeps up on Jamie's face. "I can't believe I didn't see it before."

"See what?" I ask.

"That something is going on between you and Olive."

I stand up from the couch. "There was something going on."

She stands up, studying me, and then she points a finger at me. "Oh my God! You love her."

"Yes."

"Then, what are you doing here? Go get her."

I shake my head. "It's more complicated than that."

"How so?"

"For one, she's pregnant with another man's baby."

"So?"

"Didn't you just give me some speech about how you and I couldn't be together because you wanted babies, and I didn't?"

"Yes, but Olive is different."

"How?"

"She wants the same things you do."

I run my hand through my hair. "You are frustrating, Jamie."

Jamie smiles. "I know. Now, get your ass out of my house, and go tell her that you love her."

"Five seconds ago, you told me that I should go have a threesome and that I might not even want to get married. Why would you want me to go tell Olive that I love her?"

"Because you do love her."

I feel the steam coming out of my nostrils as I listen to Jamie.

"Do you love Olive?"

"Yes."

"Then, that is all that matters. If you love her, then nothing else matters."

I pace back and forth in her room. *Jamie is crazy.*

"Do you still love me?" Jamie asks.

I stop pacing and look at her. "I love you, of course."

"But not like you love Olive," Jamie finishes for me.

I nod.

She grins. "I knew it. Go! Get out of my house!"

I grab my coat and start walking toward the door. Jamie is right. I don't know what is going on with Olive. What she is doing or if she is trying to work things out with Owen, but the problem is, I still love her, and I will do anything to stay with her.

"Where is Olive? Is she still at her apartment?" I ask Jamie.

Jamie bites her lip.

"What is it?"

"She moved out."

"What's her new address?"

Jamie thinks for a moment. "I can't tell you."

I raise an eyebrow at her. "Why the hell not?"

"Because it would be a betrayal of my friendship with her. And it's more romantic this way. It will mean more to Olive if you took the time to find her."

"Jamie, just tell me."

"No," she says with a giant smile on her face.

I sigh. "You are the most frustrating woman in the world."

I walk to the door.

"Where are you going?" Jamie asks.

"To find Olive and win her back without your help."

I hear a cheer from Jamie as I leave.

She's right. I love Olive. I want Olive. I have no idea what our future together would look like, but I have to try to find her. Wherever she is. And I know that as much as Jamie wants to help me she won't disrespect Olive's wishes. She won't tell me where Olive is.

I immediately open my phone and call one of my assistants.

"Hello Mr. Burrows," my assistant says.

"I need your help to find Olive. Call airlines. Call any relatives or friends of Olive's that you can find. Do anything and everything you can to find her? Do you understand?"

"Of course Mr. Burrows. I'll get right on it," she says.

"No, get everyone on it. Now."

I end the call and then jump into my car and race to Olive's apartment. Even though Jamie said that Olive moved I have to see for myself.

It takes me twenty minutes to get to her apartment and the entire time all I can think is please be there. Or please let a neighbor know where she is.

I pull my car over on the first available spot I can find and jump out to run inside her apartment building. I notice the no parking zone sign as soon jump out of my car but I don't care. I need to see her as soon as possible. I'll worry about my car later.

I run up the stairs and to her apartment. I knock holding my breath that she is going to come to the door. I hear footsteps and my heart races faster. The door opens and woman that is double Olive's age is standing in the doorway looking at me with annoyance.

"Yes?" she says.

I frown. "Is Olive here?" I ask hoping this woman is Olive's mother or something, but I know without asking that she isn't. She looks nothing like Olive.

"There is no Olive here," she says starting to close the door.

I grab the door. "She lived here before you. Do you know where she went?"

She glares at me. "Why the fuck would I know?"

She slams the door shut this time before I have a chance to stop her.

I run my hand through my hair. This is getting me nowhere but I have to keep trying.

I run to the next door and knock furiously, hoping that a neighbor knows where she is. I don't get an answer so I move to the next door. It opens almost immediately.

"Do you know where your old neighbor Olive moved to?" I ask.

The man frowns. "No idea."

I run to the next door and I get the same answer. I'm not going to find any answers here.

I run down the stairs while I pull out my phone to call my assistant back, hoping that in the last twenty minutes she has found something, anything for me to go on.

"Hello Mr. Burrows," she says politely when she answers.

"Do you have anything yet?" I snap.

"No sir. I'm sorry. We will keep looking."

I end the call and run back to my car. But it is no longer there. Towed most likely.

I don't have time to deal with finding it though. I call an Uber and when it arrives I tell him to go to the airport. I should get my private jet ready but I have no idea where to have it go. So it seems silly to spend all of the money and time flying form place to place endlessly until I find her.

But maybe if I just go to the airport she'll still be there. Maybe she hasn't left yet.

But after searching the airport for half an hour I know she isn't here. I try calling her but she doesn't answer her phone.

I stand in front of the ticket booth trying to figure it out. Where would a woman who has never traveled before go? Where would she go?

I have no idea.

I find myself in the ticket line inching closer to the front as I try to figure it out. When I get to the front the lady asks, "How can I help you?"

I rub my neck. "I'm not sure."

She laughs.

"I'm sorry. I should just go."

"Or you could buy a ticket to anywhere. Sometimes going somewhere is better than going nowhere."

I nod. "Where do you think I should go?"

She thinks for a second. "Well Florida is nice this time or year. Same with California. We have cheap flights to Las Vegas and Houston going on right now. I always like NYC."

"Wait...What did you just say?"

"I always like NYC."

"No, before that."

"We have cheap flights right now to Houston and Vegas."

I smile. Vegas.

My phone buzzes and I see that it is from my assistant. I answer.

"Yes."

"She's here. In Vegas," she says.

I smile. "I know. I'll be right there."

I end the call.

"I'm going to Vegas."

24

OLIVE

I have three thousand dollars in my savings account. That's it. That's everything I have to survive on before I run out of money and end up back on the streets again.

I don't have a specific plan, other than I need to get the hell out of Chicago. And I'm going to find some way to make money along the way, hopefully with something that involves the only thing I've ever really loved doing. Baking.

I sold everything that I could from my apartment, and everything I own is in a single suitcase. I'm doing this on my own. I didn't even bring Milo with me. Keri is watching him until I get settled somewhere.

I walk up to the airport counter, having no clue where I'm going.

"Hi. May I help you?" the woman says from behind the counter.

"Um...yes. I would like one ticket, please."

"To where?"

"Anywhere but here."

She laughs. "That doesn't really narrow it down for me."

"How about the cheapest flight to a decent-sized city?"

The woman types into her computer. "How about Las Vegas? We have a flight that leaves in an hour."

I nod without thinking.

Las Vegas is the last place I want to go. But then it might give me a chance to run into Sean again. And, as much as I have tried to get over him this past week, the thought of a chance encounter gets me more than a little excited.

———

Present

I've spent a week in Las Vegas, and I haven't had my chance encounter with Sean. Not that I was really expecting to run into him in a city with thousands of people, but I was hoping. It also helps that I walk by his office building every morning on my way to the small building that I got a loan to turn into a bakery.

But, every morning, when I walk by his building, I think about going inside. I think about trying to talk to him.

But I don't. Not because I'm scared, but because I don't want to destroy his life or make it more complicated.

So, instead, I just walk by. It's the best and worst part of my day. I love walking by his building. I get to think about Sean. I get to feel my heart beating rapidly in my chest again, and I get to know that there is a chance every day that the love of my life could come back into my life.

But then, every day I walk past it, I know that chance is over.

It's torture really.

I shouldn't have bought a place in Las Vegas where I'm going to have to deal with thoughts of him every single day. But I couldn't help it. It felt like destiny when I walked down the strip the first night I was in Las Vegas and found this tiny little space that was available at the far end of the strip.

In my wildest dreams, I didn't think I could get a loan for the space, but I did. Now, the only thing between me and owning my own successful bakery is a lot of hard work and a little bit of luck.

I suck in a breath as I walk past the last section of his building, like he is going to be waiting just around the corner for me. But, as I walk past the building, I know it's another day where I won't see him.

I should change my walk from where the bus drops me off over a block so that I won't have to walk past his building, but I just can't force my legs to walk a different route. Maybe after I've been here a while, I will be able to walk in this city without thinking about Sean.

I stop by my bakery shop to make sure the construction inside is going well. There isn't much that needs to happen to the space to make my bakery a reality, but a few things are needed, like a basic counter, restroom, and new flooring, before I can start operating out of it. When I am confident that everything is going well, I glance at my watch and realize it's time for my doctor's appointment.

I feel unsure about my appointment. Maybe because, once a doctor tells me I'm pregnant, then it is going to feel more real. Or maybe it's because I'm going to the appointment alone.

Keri and Jamie offered to go to my first appointment with me. But I turned them both down. It didn't seem right to go with them. This is about my journey, and I'm going to be doing this alone. So, I might as well get used to it.

I take an Uber to the doctor's office, and then I walk into the building alone. I check in and then take a seat, trying to get excited about the possibility of seeing my baby on an ultrasound.

I pull out my phone, planning on getting a head start on reading about what to expect while I'm pregnant since I have no idea what to do.

"I'm sorry," I hear a low voice next to me as someone bumps into me while taking a seat next to me.

I frown. I can't believe someone sat next to me when there are half a dozen empty seats in the waiting room.

I look up to try to figure out a reason to move when I see Sean sitting next to me with a hint of a grin.

"I'm sorry," he says again.

"For what?" I ask.

"For not telling you this sooner. I love you, Olive. I realize that I never actually said those words to you before. That's probably why it was so easy for you to believe that I could be in love with a woman other than you. But I can't. I only love you, Olive. Crazy, goofy, gorgeous you."

I feel a tear roll down my cheek.

"I'm sorry that I let you walk out of my office without running after you.

"I'm sorry that I didn't call you every night since then.

"I'm sorry I almost let you go to a doctor's appointment by yourself.

"I'm sorry that I never believed in us. I do now. And, if you're willing to give me a second chance, I would love to spend however long you'd be mine making it up to you."

I smile. "I'm not sorry."

He frowns in disappointment.

"I'm not sorry that you were an ass to me when we first met.

"I'm not sorry that I hated you initially.

"I'm not sorry that I fucked you too many times to count.

"I'm not sorry that I quit my job.

"I'm not sorry about any of it because it got me to this point."
He nods.

"Olive," I hear the nurse shout.

I stand up and start walking toward her with a smile on my face, but I don't feel Sean walking behind me.

I glance over my shoulder and see Sean is still sitting in the chair in the waiting room, looking disappointed.

"You're going to have something else to be sorry about if you don't get your ass up and come with me to my appointment."

Sean laughs as he gets up and follows me into one of the exam rooms.

"Lie back on the table. The doctor will be in and will want to do an ultrasound first. Then, he will go from there," the nurse says before she leaves.

Sean looks at me as I climb up onto the table. "You still love me?"

I laugh. "Yes, you goof, I still love you. I thought that was clear."

He shakes his head and then kisses me hard on the lips as his hands travel down my body to my hips. Sean slowly stops kissing and looks down at my stomach and then up into my eyes. "I'll love this baby like it's my own. Don't worry about that," he says reassuringly.

I smile. He's right. I know he will. And I'll love this baby, too. I'm just still getting used to the idea.

We hear a knock on the door, followed by the doctor entering.

"Let's take a good look at how your baby is doing," the doctor says.

I nod and lie back as the doctor gets the ultrasound equipment together. I lift my shirt up, and he places the instrument on my stomach. I take a deep breath as I stare at the screen, waiting for the first image of my baby. But my eyes quickly go to the doctor, who is humming a little to himself, taking his sweet time with finding my baby.

Another minute passes, and the doctor still doesn't say anything. I glance over at Sean, who grabs hold of my hand and looks awfully nervous himself.

"Is something wrong?" Sean asks because I can't get any words out.

"Please sit up for a moment," the doctor says.

I sit up without bothering to wipe the goop off my stomach first. I don't care. I just need answers.

"When did you take a pregnancy test?" the doctor asks.

I think for a moment. "About two weeks ago."

"How many tests did you take then?"

"Just the one." I dig into my purse, pull out my phone with the picture I took of the positive pregnancy test, and show the doctor.

The doctor laughs and visibly relaxes. "I was worried that you'd had a miscarriage, and that is always hard news to break to someone because pregnancy tests these days are almost always accurate. But looking at this picture shows that isn't true."

"What do you mean?" I ask, not understanding.

"I'm so sorry, Olive, but you aren't pregnant. You just read the test wrong."

My eyes shoot wide open, and a grin creeps over my face. "I'm not pregnant?" I say, not believing it.

"I'm sorry again, but you're not pregnant. I'll give you two a few moments alone," the doctor says, getting up.

I turn to Sean. "I'm not pregnant."

"Are you okay with that?" he asks hesitantly, not sure what to say.

I laugh. "I'm more than okay with it."

He laughs and scoops me up in his arms, spinning me around. "I can't believe you read the test wrong. Let me see."

I show him the image on my phone.

He laughs. "Two pink lines mean you're pregnant. One line means you're not."

I blush. "I read the instructions quickly."

Sean shakes his head. "I love you even though you're always going to keep me on my toes."

I smile. "You'd better."

"So, what now? What do you want, Olive?"

I think for a moment. "I want you to use that butt plug like you did in Anal Adventures 3."

Sean laughs. "So, you watched some of my porn movies?"

I bite my lip. "I needed something to get me through these last couple of weeks."

Sean kisses me. "I'll give you anything you want. Babies, houses, jets, and of course, all the sex you could ever want."

"What if I just want the sex and put a hold on all the rest? Would you regret going out with me if it meant that you might be giving up the mansion and two-point-five kids?" I ask, not sure how he is going to respond.

"As long as I have you, that's all that matters."

He kisses me again, and I lose myself in the kiss. I want him. Now. But we are in an exam room. We have to make it to one of our apartments first.

"We need to stop," I say.

"Why?"

"Because you can't fuck me in a doctor's office," I whisper, like the room is bugged and someone can hear us.

But Sean grins, and I forget about everything else.

"I think you want me to fuck you right here, right now," Sean says.

I bite my lip and try to shake my head, but I end up nodding.

The next thing I know, Sean has me bent over the exam room, and his cock is pushing inside my pussy while I try my best to be as quiet as I can. But, of course, I can't stay quiet. I scream Sean's name, and three seconds later, there is a knock on the door, followed by one of the nurses poking her head in, probably to make sure I'm okay.

"Oh my God! You can't do that in here!" she shouts at us.

Sean slips out of me, and I quickly pull my pants back up.

"Get out!" she screams.

Sean grabs my hand, and we run out of the room and don't stop until we are outside.

I suck in a breath. "I think I'm going to have to change doctors," I say, laughing.

Sean laughs, too, before pulling me toward him and softly kissing me on the lips.

"I'm sorry we got caught. But you were such a dirty girl that I couldn't resist."

I bite my lip. "I'm not."

EPILOGUE

SEAN

O̴ne Year Later

"Hey baby, what's the emergency?" I ask, as I enter her new bakery shop. It's her second bakery and it's opening in three days, hence the emergency text message I got this morning.

I look at Olive covered in flour standing in her kitchen. I know she's stressed and needs help, but I can't help but get turned on when I see her living her dream and being so successful at it. I know she has her doubts, which are always good to have when starting something new but she has no reason to worry. Her last bakery has done better than either of us ever imagined. This second location is going to do just as well and after this, the sky is the limit.

She grins when she sees me, like just my presence here takes away all of the stress.

She stops pouring the batter into the cupcake tins and walks over and kisses me on the lips.

"I'm so glad you are here," she says.

I grab her neck and kiss her again. She melts into my arms as I kiss her and take away her anxiety. I wish I could just spend the rest of today kissing her, but I know that I shouldn't. She needs to work.

"How can I help?" I finally ask, tearing my lips away from hers.

Her eyes grow wide and the expression on her face is one of guilt.

"What is it?" I ask cautiously.

"I need you to help me bake some things for tomorrow. I'm catering for a large wedding and I need help."

I frown. "What happened to the other bakers?"

She bites her lip. "They called in sick."

I narrow my eyes as I study hers. "You let them all have the same day off again, didn't you?"

She kisses me softly on the lips to keep me from scolding her.

"They deserved it. They've been working hard," she says.

"And what about you?"

She grins. "I have you to help." She throws me an apron.

I sigh but put it on. "I'll help but I can't promise I'll be any better than the last time. You'd be better off just baking everything yourself."

Her face lights up as she looks at me. "But then I wouldn't get to see you looking so hot in your apron."

She pinches my ass before returning to baking.

I groan. "Fine. I'll help you, but only if I get to fuck you in nothing but your apron later."

She bites her lip again. "Deal."

She gives me a task and I try to focus on it instead of on her ass, but she makes it impossible. She rubs up against me every chance she gets. She smears flour on my face at least half a dozen times. She sways her hips even more than usual when she walks. Little whimpers and sounds leave her lips while she is working.

I break, faster than I would like. Olive drives me insane with need on a normal day much less when she is trying to drive me mad.

I grab her and push her against the wall, pushing her hands high above her head.

"What are you doing?" I ask as I stare intently into her eyes.

She breathes heavily. "Getting you to fuck me."

I raise an eyebrow. "Well, that's easy. All you have to do is ask."

She grins. "I want you to fuck me here."

I see the naughtiest look in her eyes when she says it.

I don't think about the fact of how unhygienic it is to fuck in her bakery's kitchen. I'll have a cleaning crew come in later.

"Tell me what you want Olive," I say because I know her. She has a plan in her head.

She takes a deep breath. "I want you to fuck me on the counter."

I grab her and give her what she wants. I lift her up, wrapping her legs around me as I kiss her. She claws at my back as I sit her on the counter before grabbing her jeans and pulling them off at the same time that she undoes her apron and pulls it off. I grab the hem of her shirt and yank it off of her head.

Olive pushes her body back onto the table and that's when I get a full look at the lingerie she is wearing. She planned this. There was no emergency. The emergency was that she needed to get fucked.

I glance around the room until I spot it. The video camera that she set up.

I laugh and shake my head. "So which porno is this that we

are reenacting?" I ask. She's been trying to get me to come out of retirement and make a porn movie with her. Just a private one.

She blushes. "The one where you fuck me in my bakery."

I shake my head but then I climb on top of her anyway. I would do anything for her. Even recreate a cheesy porn movie with her if that is what she wants.

I kiss down her neck and then unclasp her bra.

She arches her back and moans loudly as I do, exaggerating everything for the camera. I'm going to make it the best sex of her life then.

I move my lips down her body until I reach her red lace panties. I bite the band of her panties with my teeth and pull them down slowly as Olive stares at me, waiting for the moment that my tongue moves inside her.

I hesitate, letting her anticipation build as I hover over her. Then I lick her pussy and she screams.

But it's not her usual scream. This scream is terrifying.

I stop immediately, sitting up and pulling her to me to find out what is wrong. I see the blood and panic.

It's a lot of blood. Too much blood oozing down her arm.

"What happened?" I ask, as I grab the nearest clean dish towel and grab her hand to apply pressure to her wound that is most definitely going to need stitches.

She winces when I wrap the towel around her hand.

"I was trying to grab onto something because what you were doing felt so good... I think I grabbed a knife."

"I know we will laugh about this later but right now I need to get you to the emergency room. I think you need stitches."

She nods and I help her get dressed and then into my car so that I can rush her to the emergency room. As soon as we are both in the car, I step on the gas to get her to the emergency room.

"Slow down Sean," she says.

"No. I need to get you help," I say speeding up instead of slowing down.

"Sean. Stop," she says more firmly and I sigh but slow down a little.

I look at her to make sure that the bleeding hasn't gotten worse. I know it's only a cut on her hand but it's deep and I don't know what I would do without her. I don't think I could survive without her.

"Why are you looking at me like that?" she asks.

I shake my head. "I'll tell you after we are finished."

We make it to the hospital and after waiting twenty minutes in the waiting room, far longer than I was happy with, Olive was finally brought back to a room where they stitched up her hand.

"So how did this happen?" the doctor asks Olive when he finishes stitching her up.

She looks at me and blushes but says, "Baking accident."

He nods. "Well, you should be all better now. Hopefully we won't see you back for any more baking accidents," he says emphasizing the last words and looking at me like he knows what really happened even though he couldn't know.

He finally leaves us alone in the room and I kiss Olive's forehead. "I'm so glad you are okay. I was worried about you."

She laughs. "You need to stop freaking out every time something like this happens. I'm a klutz. Stuff like this happens to me all the time. If you are going to be with me you need to be used to going to the emergency room."

"I'll never get used to you being in pain or almost dying."

She shakes her head. "You're over exaggerating. I didn't almost die."

"I know. It was still hard to watch you go through that much pain."

"What did you want to tell me earlier in the car?" she asks.

I look at her in the eye and know that this is the wrong place and the wrong way to do this but I don't have a choice. I have to tell her how I feel.

"That I want to marry you," I say.

Her eyes widen a little but she doesn't seem that shocked that I would ask. We've been dating for a year. We love each other. It's the next natural step.

But she doesn't say anything. She doesn't show excitement or say that she wants to marry me too.

"What do you think? Will you marry me? Or do you want to wait to answer until I do it right? Get a ring and find some romantic place?"

"Why do you want to marry me?" she asks.

I frown. "Because I love you and I want to spend the rest of my life with you."

She nods. "I love you and want to spend the rest of my life with you too but it doesn't mean that we should get married."

"Shouldn't it?" I ask.

She smiles. "I don't need to get married to know that you love me and will do anything for me for the rest of your life. One look today from you when my hand was cut was all it took to know that I'm yours forever."

"And I'm yours forever." I study her closely. "Will you marry me?" I ask again.

Her face lights up. "Yes. I'll marry you, but only because I want an excuse to go on a long honeymoon where you can fuck me in a dozen countries."

I grin. "God, I love you," I say kissing her.

Olive is mine. I'm going to make it official by marrying her. And then take her on a year long honeymoon. I know she can find the right bakers to handle her bakeries while we are gone.

After all, I was the one that taught her everything I know. She's going to kill this running a business thing. She already is. She's everything I never knew I wanted in a woman and more. And she's all fucking mine. Forever.

THE END

ALSO BY ELLA MILES

My next release is going to be Heart of a Liar and is going to be included exclusively in the Hot & Sinful Nights boxset! You get over 20 HOT romances for 99 cents when you Pre Order today!! Coming September 26th

Pre Order Hot & Sinful Nights

Read More by Ella Miles Here

BONUS COLORING PAGE

Get your bonus coloring page here—> https://www.ellamiles.-com/downloads/NotSorry_coloringbook.pdf

ABOUT ELLA MILES

Ella Miles writes steamy romance with a twist. She's currently living her own happily ever after near the Rocky Mountains with her high school sweetheart husband. Her heart is also taken by her goofy four year old black lab that is scared of everything, including her own shadow.

Ella is the author of the bestselling book: TOO MUCH. She is also the author of the ALIGNED series, MAYBE series, DEFINITELY series, and UNFORGIVABLE series. Get a free book by visiting her website: EllaMiles.com/freebooks.

Stalk her at:

www.ellamiles.com
ella@ellamiles.com

ACKNOWLEDGMENTS

This book was really fun to write and was a bit different than any other book I've written. I came up with the idea for a book at a time when I didn't have time to actually write it. So instead of taking a month or two and just writing it straight through I started writing a chapter a week or whenever I could fit it in between other projects. And then I posted the book to my website for anyone to read and give feedback on as I wrote it.

It was such a fun experience to write it this way and to read everyone's feedback as I wrote it! I might even do it again with another book in the future.

So first and foremost I must thank everyone that read that initial version of this book! You are all amazing and it so nice to hear how excited you all were to read another chapter each week.

To everyone that not only read it but also gave me feedback both positive and negative thank you! You really helped me figure out how to make this book the best that it can be! Thank you to Debbie C., Abigail A., Maj B., Marion M., Colleen D., Terry A., Cheryl M., Tannie L., Crystal C., Tina P., Linda L., Lenora S., Caliestro N., Jennifer K., and Tracey.

I know I'm probably forgetting someone and for that I'm sorry! If I forgot you, remind me so that I can make it right! :)

I must thank my wonderful editor Jovana. You are amazing and I don't know how you put up with me missing deadlines and all the horrible typos that I make, especially now that I'm dictating more. You're amazing!!

Thank you Cara for making me a beautiful cover as always!!

Thank you to my husband who put up with me while I wrote this and also helped me with the final round of proofreading! Maybe someday I'll write something with less romance in it that you actually want to read instead of being forced into reading :) Thank you for reading my books anyway! I love you.

And thank you to my readers! You are all so so amazing!! This has been an incredible journey so far and I can't wait to see what comes. Thank you!!

www.ingramcontent.com/pod-product-compliance
Lightning Source LLC
Chambersburg PA
CBHW050405190726

48284CB00007BB/2445